The Best of African FOLKLORE

PHYLLIS SAVORY

Illustrated by
Gina Daniel

The Best of African FOLKLORE

PHYLLIS SAVORY

Illustrated by
Gina Daniel

CONTENTS

JABULANI AND THE LION

SWAZI

Jabulani was pleased with life. He sang happily to himself as he walked through the forest. Soon he approached a big log trap built by one of the hunters in his village. A plaintive voice called to him as he passed, "Jabulani, my friend, please set me free. I am dying from hunger and thirst."

The boy was kind at heart, and always ready to help those in trouble – but this was a lion in the trap, and helping a lion was an entirely different matter. "If I let you out," he said, "you'll probably be so hungry that you'll eat me!"

"Oh no, I'd never do such a dreadful thing! I promise most faithfully I will not eat you. Now please have pity on me and let me out," pleaded the lion.

"Well," said the tender-hearted boy, "since I have your faithful promise, I will help you." So he lifted the heavy door that had fallen when the lion entered the trap, tempted in by the bait.

The lion backed out and stretched his cramped limbs. Then he yawned, "Come along. I need a good long drink at the river before I eat you."

"But you promised!" the boy reminded him, now mighty scared.

"Promises don't count when you're as hungry as I am," was the lion's answer as he bared his cruel yellow fangs.

"But please," begged Jabulani, "let's be fair about this! Let's ask all the other animals if it's right for you to go back on your word. Let them decide."

"Oh, very well," agreed the lion, and the two walked down to the river for the lion to have a drink. There they met a sad old donkey.

"Friend donkey," said the boy, "please give us your opinion. There is a desperate disagreement between Lord Lion and me. I found him securely caught in a trap and he begged me to set him free. He promised faithfully that if I did, he wouldn't eat me. So I did set him free and now he says that he will eat me. Is this fair?"

The donkey chewed thoughtfully for a few minutes before he replied, "Yes, it's quite fair for him to eat you, for you humans have no pity on us animals. When I was young and useful to my master, he cared for me, and how cheerfully I carried his loads upon my back. He gave me good food, and treated me with kindness; but now that I am too old to work, he has driven me out to die of starvation, for my old teeth are too worn to cope with the tough winter grass.

6

Why should humans deserve pity? I agree with Lord Lion. You should be eaten."

The lion was opening his mouth when the boy hurriedly pointed out, "That's only one animal's opinion. We must ask them all." Rather grudgingly, the lion agreed.

The next animal they met was a cow, and Jabulani told her what had happened. She shook her horned head angrily. "Humans!" she said. "You are all the same. We give our milk willingly for you to drink, and we even pull ploughs so you can plant your crops. But when our useful years are past, what happens? You kill and eat us, and use our hides for clothes. Surely it's perfectly fair that you should now provide a meal. I agree with my lord the lion. You should be eaten." And she pawed the ground with her hoof.

"But there are other animals," said the boy, now badly frightened, "the wild creatures. There are hundreds of animals and we've only heard two of them. You did agree we should ask them all."

"Oh, well," grumbled the lion, "as you wish, but do hurry. I'm getting more hungry every minute. They'll all be on my side."

Then down the path trotted another lion. Jabulani repeated his story.

"Now listen, human," roared the second lion. "Day by day my life is in danger from people like you. I can't take a drink at the river without glancing over my shoulder all the time to be sure a spear is not hurtling towards me from some crafty hunter. How can we live in peace with worries like that? Surely, it's quite fair for my brother to eat you!"

"But please, friend lion – for you called me 'friend' before I released you," begged Jabulani, trembling, "let's ask the antelopes. They are wild animals too." But one after the other the antelopes condemned the human race.

"We live in fear of our lives," they said, "because of your hunters and their dogs. All they want is to kill us because they are hungry. Isn't it fair for you to provide a meal now for an animal who is hungry?"

By this time poor Jabulani had given up hope of ever seeing his home again, since all the animals thought he should be eaten. Then he saw a jackal slinking along one of the animal paths that crisscrossed the forest. "Uncle Jackal," he called, "of all the wild animals, you're the only one who hasn't given us his opinion." Once more he went through the whole story of how he had set the lion free. "Is it fair that in return for my kindness, he should eat me?" Jabulani asked.

The jackal thought for several minutes before replying. Then he shook his head and put on a very stupid expression. "It's very difficult to make up my mind, Jabulani," he said, "because I don't understand how the lion came to be in the trap. Let's go to the trap, all three of us, so I can see what you mean." So the lion and Jabulani led the jackal to the trap.

"Now," said the jackal turning to the lion, "where exactly were you, when you called to Jabulani to help you? Were you actually inside the trap?"

"Yes," answered the lion, "I was inside the trap."

"But I can't understand how, or why you got there. Show me how you got in."

The lion walked into the trap, but the jackal pretended he was still not satisfied. "Was the trap open or closed?" he asked.

"Closed," said the lion, snarling at the memory.

"Well, close it, Jabulani, so that I can see exactly what you mean," went on the jackal. The boy took the hint at once and, as the heavy door fell into place, the jackal said, "Good bye, Foolish One! This time you can stay there till you die. It certainly isn't fair to reward good with evil, however hungry you are."

Jabulani thanked the jackal with tears in his eyes for saving his life so cleverly that the lion received his own fair reward.

・　・　・　・　・

There is an old Swazi saying: *No one is clever enough to eat the meat from his own back!*

LUNGILE AND THE BEWITCHED BUCK

SWAZI

No girl was more beautiful than Lungile; and no girl was more loved by those around her. She was hard-working, too, so that her lobola, her bride-price, was high; so high, in fact, that none but the son of a chief could afford the hundred cows that her father demanded. But for some time now, there had been great activity and preparations in her father's kraal, for she was to become the chosen "first wife" of the son of a wealthy neighbouring chief, and her wedding garment was almost ready for her to wear. For weeks her devoted father had been working on the ox-hide from which her wedding-dress was being fashioned. First he had pounded it with the utmost care until it was soft and supple; then had come the rubbing with charcoal and fat, to give the desired jet-black colour required for the wedding garment of every Swazi maid.

This, of course, was only the beginning; now came her mother's turn, and no one in all the land was more cunning in the cutting and shaping of a robe of such importance. To begin with, it had to fit snugly around the waist and hips, after which the real skill had to be shown in the graceful folds in which it hung about the knees; an expert's work, indeed. But at last it was completed, and the bridal attendants were waiting only for the word from Lungile before they would creep silently away at dawn on the chosen day. No one must know the day or the hour of their departure, for goodbyes are avoided by a Swazi bride on the day she leaves her home.

It was to be a long journey, but Lungile's heart was full of gladness as the party left at cock-crow on a summer morning. Not only was she going to the home of a kind and noble chief, but her groom was good and handsome, and already she loved him dearly. Besides this, she was well aware that she was by far the most beautiful maiden in the land, so she felt sure of a warm welcome to her new home. Did she not grow the finest crops in her father's land, and brew beer that was unequalled for miles around? That she was desirable had been proved beyond doubt, by the number of young men who had wanted to marry her. Life was indeed good, and joyful were the marriage songs that the party sang as they journeyed on their way.

Yes, it was a long, long way, but eventually they reached the bridegroom's kraal. There they were received with honour and songs of welcome, as they were shown into the spacious quarters that had been prepared for them. Lungile's cup of happiness was full. And there was more to come: two beautiful jet-black oxen arrived. These were to provide the meat for the marriage feast. "The best," the old chief had ordered, "in all my herd."

All was bustle and excitement on the following morning, as the men prepared the meat for roasting on the glowing embers that had been smouldering since dawn, and Lungile watched the preparations from her hut with pride. Juicy steaks were handed to the bridegroom's mother, who in no time had them sizzling merrily upon the embers. Pots of the finest beer were arranged in the place set aside for the feast, and all was running smoothly when, to the horror of the chief's wife, the meat began to leap and twist, as though objecting to the heat. Never before in her long life, had the old chieftainess seen such a dreadful happening, and she ran in haste to call her husband. But when she returned, she found that the skins, heads, and every morsel of the meat had vanished. Not even a spot of fat remained spitting on the embers.

"This smells of witchery!" exclaimed the chief, looking suspiciously in the direction of Lungile's hut but, calling for his son he said, "Send for the perfect white bull that came as your sister's bridal price, ten moons ago. His purity should dispel all evil on an occasion such as this!" and the bridegroom lost no time in carrying out his father's order.

After her first gasp of dismay at what had taken place, Lungile calmed herself as she saw the beautiful white bull being driven in at the kraal gate. "Surely, no honour could be greater than this," she thought with relief. And truly, it was a noble beast; no spot spoiled its perfect skin, and she watched delightedly as it tossed its long black horns, and picked its way delicately through the stubble – its hoofs as shiny black as its horns.

It was not long before the lovely beast was killed and cut up, but this time the chief's wife decided not to grill, but to boil the meat, and she therefore prepared an enormous pot of steaming water, and into it she plunged the noble beast's head. Again all seemed to be going well, when out of the pot there suddenly jumped a young man as handsome as a prince. Just as suddenly, he turned into a cream-coloured buck, sprang over the fence that enclosed the kraal and disappeared into the nearby forest.

"Send the witch home!" cried the chief in consternation. "She has brought disaster and disgrace upon our people. Drive the wicked girl back to her people; no son of mine will be married to a sorceress. See, too, that her father sends back the hundred fat cows that I paid for her lobola!"

Poor Lungile tried to assure the chief and his people that she was innocent of any evil intentions towards either his family or his tribe – nor had she had anything to do with these strange happenings. However, all her tears were in vain and, with sticks and stones, the would-be bride and her attendants were driven from his land.

It was a sad party that travelled the long way home, and for many weeks the broken-hearted girl kept to her hut, ashamed and dejected. But the months wore on, and then the years, until eventually her old light-hearted happiness returned to her, and once more she became the most hard-working maiden in the land. But news of the strange happenings at her wedding feast had spread throughout the country, and now no young men came to seek her hand, for none wished to risk such a happening again.

One day, however, while she was hoeing the crops in her father's land, she felt a strange presence near to her and, looking up, saw an incredibly beautiful cream-coloured buck watching her intently. "Where," she wondered, "have I seen this animal before?" It came towards her and circled round the land she hoed. At first she took no notice, and continued with her work – but after a while she looked up again and there it was, apparently trying to attract her attention.

"Maybe I could catch it," she thought to herself, "it seems to be so tame." She put down her hoe and went towards it. "It must be the lovely creature that ran into the forest at my wedding feast. I will see if I can kill it: that would be a fitting punishment for the mischief it has brought me." And so the chase began.

In and out of the criss-cross paths at the forest edge they dodged, with the buck keeping just out of reach all the time. Sometimes it allowed her to touch it, but never was she able to hold it. The lovely creature led her further and further into the forest, and more than once she was about to turn, for the evening was closing in – but each time the buck circled round and tempted her to follow, until at last it allowed her to catch it by the horns.

For a delicate and elegant creature, it proved to be stronger than she had thought possible. However, she kept her grip, hoping, as it pulled her along the path, that she would meet a hunter from her kraal who would help her to capture the buck. But no help appeared, and soon she found that they were in more open country; huge forest-clad mountains with beautiful valleys between them stretched ahead and the girl realised that the shadows had lengthened alarmingly, so that if she did not return at once, she would be forced to spend the night in this lonely place.

"This chase must stop!" said Lungile aloud and, releasing her hold of the buck's horns, fled back along the path towards her home. After she had gone a short distance, she felt compelled to stop and look back. There, following her was the same lovely buck. It had such a sad, appealing look in its big brown eyes, that a feeling of great pity came over her. "Are you in trouble?" she asked. "Can I help you?" It never altered its position, so she walked up to it, and again caught it by the horns.

"If you are prepared to help me," the buck replied, "you must show no fear in what lies ahead of us, and do all that I ask of you,"

"Surely this must be a magical buck," thought the girl to herself, "for he speaks as one of us," and aloud she answered, "I will do your bidding, lovely creature, because I can see that you are in, trouble."

11

"Then follow me," replied the buck as, turning, he picked his way delicately towards the forest clad mountains. Before long they came to a gurgling boulder-strewn stream, where Lungile started back in horror at the sight of a terrible ogre, who was sitting on one of the boulders. His enormous pointed eye-teeth hung over his bottom lip almost to his chin, and round his brow he wore a band of animals' eyes. In one hand he held a rope tied round the neck of a hideous and enormous hyena.

"Ah!" said the ogre, turning to the hyena, "We don't need to go hunting today. Here is plenty of meat!" And he hastened forward to grab the buck. The buck, however, made no attempt to move and, as the ogre's hand touched him, it turned into a handsome young man, who

seized the wicked creature by the throat and threw him to the ground. The hyena, seeing his master overpowered ran, with its tail between its legs, screaming into the forest, never to be seen again. The young man meanwhile, during what seemed to the girl a struggle that lasted forever, finally strangled the dreadful ogre.

As the ogre died, the circlet of animals' eyes, which had fallen from his head, turned back into gentle buck. They now came crowding round to nuzzle and caress the young man, their master. "These are my people," said the young man to Lungile. "For I am the son of a chief. Many years ago a wicked king turned me into a white bull to lead his herd of noble cattle, and all my people were turned into buck, to roam the forests of my kingdom until they and I were freed of the curse. You have set me free, and now, sweet one, we must rescue my people."

"Tell me what to do," replied Lungile, her eyes shining with the love she already felt for this handsome young man.

"You must stay among my people in this wild region, and every day you must go out to gather spinach, and you must call to them with this magic song:

> 'Buck, buck, come down from the hills;
> Your leader is a man once again.
> He was changed to an animal, as you were:
> Come down and be changed into men!'"

"But how did it happen that you were killed for my marriage feast, three long years ago?" asked Lungile.

"Having changed me into a white bull, the wicked king sent me to lead the herd which was paid as the bride-price for the sister of the man you were to marry," answered the chief's son. "But grieve no more, my lovely one, that you lost your bridegroom, for if you will marry me, I will give you greater happiness and riches than would have been in his power to offer." There was no need for him to wait for her reply for her eyes told him all that he wished to know.

For many days now, Lungile stayed among the buck in the forest, gathering spinach daily while she sang the magic song, while from far and near the buck came in answer to the song; old buck, young buck, and tiny fawns. All gathered round her, waiting expectantly; then, one morning, as the rising sun sent its first rays of brilliance over the hilltops, they were all changed into men, women and children – and, as though shrouded in the early morning mist, the chief's son himself came striding through the forest, to claim them as his long lost tribe.

It was a happy home-coming for Lungile, and the celebrations that followed were splendid.

Never did a bride have a kinder or more loving husband, and never was such a magnificent herd of cows presented to a proud father, as her "bride-price". And, as the years passed, many were the children who played around their happy home.

MONTUAI AND THE HYENA
SWAZI

Montuai's father was proud of his crop of mealies. The cobs were swelling daily, and he was sure he would have a good harvest – if only he could keep the birds away. They kept coming now to pick the juicy grain and more of them every day. For several days he himself had chased them away but, he decided, this was not a grown man's work. "Surely Montuai is now old enough to do such work," he thought. He therefore built a small hut in which to keep her food and to shelter her from rain and, preparing a pot of food for her breakfast and midday meal, he sent off his small daughter at sunrise each day to chase away the troublesome birds.

It was lonely work for the little girl, as she had no brother or sister to keep her company. She sang to herself to ease the loneliness as she ran from one side of the field to the other, while the birds flocked here and there. At meal times she went to the little hut her father had built for her.

She was about to begin her breakfast one day, when she heard a harsh voice calling, "Montuai, Montuai!" She ran to the door, thinking that a human called, but to her distress she saw an evil-looking hyena by the far side of the mealie field.

"What do you want?" she asked nervously.

"I want you to come and carry me to your hut," replied the dreadful beast.

"You are too heavy for me to lift," answered the child. "Why cannot you use your own legs?" "I dislike wetting my feet in the early morning dew," growled the hyena. "Obey me at once," he added, "or I will eat you!" So the poor child had no choice but to go across the field, pick up the horrid animal and carry him to her hut.

"Who does this belong to?" he asked, lifting the lid from the pot and sniffing inside. "It is my father's food," replied Montuai.

"Oh ho," said the hyena, "if it is not my food, I will have to eat you."

"Well, eat it," sobbed the child terrified, and the hyena emptied the pot. Then to her great relief, he went to the river to drink.

That evening when she went home, Montuai told her father that an ugly animal from the forest had frightened her. "I shall come tomorrow and see what it is," he told her, but he forgot, and she had to go to the mealie-field alone when the morning came. She had not been in her little hut for long, before she again heard the same voice calling "Montuai, Montuai!"

"Yes," she answered, shaking with fear.

"Come and carry me to your hut at once!" the hyena ordered, and, trembling in every limb, she was forced to obey the dreadful animal. He took the lid off her pot and asked as before, "Who does this belong to?"

"As I said yesterday, it belongs to my father," said the child.

"As I said yesterday," sneered the hyena, copying her, "if it is not my food, I will have to eat you."

And again he ate all the food in the pot before going to the river to drink.

That evening Montuai complained once more to her father about the animal from the forest, but he told her that she must be imagining things, and sent her alone to the mealie-field the next morning.

The hyena, pleased he had found a meal every day so easily, saw the child enter her hut with the pot of food and he called out at once, "Montuai, Montuai!" She was too frightened to do anything but run out and carry him to her hut.

For the third time he took the lid off the pot and asked the same question: "Who does this belong to?"

"It is my father's," sobbed Montuai.

"Well, if it is not my food, I shall certainly eat you," he said, drawing back his lips to show his yellow fangs as he came towards her.

"No, no! It is your food," screamed the child. "Please eat it," and for the third time the hyena emptied the pot before going to the river to drink.

That evening Montuai told her father that she would rather be beaten than go again alone to the mealie-field. So on the following morning, taking a hoe with him, he went with her, and hid behind some bundles of thatching grass in the hut.

Not long after their arrival, she heard the dreaded voice calling again. But this time when the hyena told her to come and fetch him she refused. "Come by yourself! I'm not carrying you today."

"I told you I don't like getting my feet wet. Come at once!" he growled.

"Coward!" called Montuai, laughing. So, forced to walk to the hut on his own two feet, the hyena was very angry. "I'll deal with you properly when I have eaten. Now tell me, who does that food belong to? Is it mine?"

"No," answered the girl defiantly – no longer afraid, now that her father was near, "it is my father's!"

"When I have finished it, you will suffer for your cheek," he threatened, taking off the lid and putting his head into the pot. He was so pleased with the delicious food inside, that he did not see Montuai's father creep from his hiding place, raise his hoe and strike. He did not even know what had hit him as he fell with a deep wound on the back of his neck.

The father dragged the ugly beast's body out of the hut, and left him under some bushes, thinking he was dead. Montuai, no longer afraid, settled down to her work of scaring the birds from the ripening mealies once more. Nor had she any fear as she went singing to the mealie-field early on the following morning. But imagine her terror when she arrived, for the hyena, his neck covered in blood, was waiting for her at the end of the field.

"Montuai, Montuai!" he called. "Come and carry me to your hut!"

The poor child did not dare to disobey. She picked up the horrible creature and carried him to her hut. She put the food down in front of him and she said, "It is yours; eat it."

When the pot had been licked clean the hyena said, "Now, wash the wound your father made on my neck – and be quick about it – for this time I am going to carry you to the river, where I will drown you in the big pool."

With trembling hands Montuai cleaned the gash on the hyena's neck. After she had done so, he picked her up and, putting her upon his back, began a slow jog-trot to the river. His wound was hurting him, so he kept his nose to the ground, and did not look to right or left as he went.

"What can I do to escape?" thought Montuai. Fortunately she had a quick mind, and soon she saw a heavy forked branch lying on the path ahead. She caught hold of it as they passed and put it over the hyena's shoulders in front of her. Then she slipped quietly off over his tail. On and on jogged the hyena, still looking neither right nor left, until he reached the pool where he had planned to drown Montuai. Standing at the edge of the water, he jerked his load into the deep pool. The heavy thud of the branch as it splashed into the water made him look round, but all he saw was the forked branch of a tree floating where the girl should have been.

His howl of rage echoed far and wide, and he ran back to find her. But he was far too late, for Montuai had lost no time in running home as fast as her legs would carry her. And she never went back to chase the birds from the ripening mealies, for her father watched them for the few days that were left before he gathered in his crop.

For two days the hyena wandered about with his nose to the ground, looking neither to the right nor to the left, for the wound on his neck made it so stiff that he couldn't move it at all. That meant that he couldn't hunt for food either, so on the third day he died – and nobody was sorry!

Narrator: A.S. Cambul.

THE WHITE DOVE

SWAZI

Of all the hunters in the land, the most skilled of them all was the king's only son, Sanfu, and no one loved hunting so much. He would leave the Royal Kraal with his knobkerries and spears to enjoy a day's hunting, for his father's country was rich in game of every kind. Seldom did he return without a kill slung over his shoulder for his family to eat.

One fateful morning he left home when the day was crisp with sunshine: ideal hunting weather. But for some unknown reason prize after prize escaped him. Was his skill slipping? he wondered, annoyed, as he missed one throw after another. Buck were there as usual, but he failed to bring them down, as he followed them for hour after hour. Even the hare and smaller animals seemed determined to escape, while they led him farther and farther from his home, until he found himself in a strange country which he had never seen before.

He was about to turn for home when he saw ahead of him two high twin peaks, with tall forests reaching to their grass-covered tops. Surely this should be a hunter's paradise, he thought as he pressed on – and up, up, up he climbed through the trees. So dense were their branches that the sun was hidden from sight, while underfoot he trod on soft, moss-covered ground, where his footsteps made no sound. Birds of every colour darted here and there, while monkey-chatter from the huge creepers that hung from above was the only sound that broke the silence. Yes, there was game here, too, but try as he might, he caught only fleeting glimpses of their stately horns as the buck kept out of range of his spears, vanishing as if by magic.

Sanfu eventually decided to try the open lands above, where there were no trees to spoil his view, so he continued to clamber upwards. He soon found himself at the top of a grass-covered pass between the mountains, where he looked into a valley of immense size and majestic beauty. "Surely I must find something here," he thought, as he began the downward climb. But to his surprise he found that it was far more difficult going down than it had been climbing up, for the ground was covered with hundreds of rocks and boulders that gave way and rolled with him down the slope.

Bumped and bruised from his fall, he stood up and looked around. The grass was so high that it hid any game there might be. Disappointed, he turned wearily to retrace his steps, but to his surprise found that tall forbidding cliffs had arisen behind him, completely barring his return. So steep were they, that he realised that there was no other way he could go except on down to the valley beneath.

By this time it was getting late, and he had had nothing to eat or drink since he left home, so he was both hungry and thirsty. There had been no sign of human life. Such a deep and sinister silence hung around him, that he decided he must surely be in the land of spirits.

While he was wondering what to do next, he was startled by the sound of soft footsteps. A few paces behind him stood an old, old woman, clothed from head to foot in a long black cloak. In her right hand she held a tall black staff, on top of which were perched two black ravens.

"Mother," Sanfu addressed her politely, when he had recovered from his surprise, "I am far from home, and in a strange land. Can you tell me where I may find food, water and shelter for the night?"

The old woman put her finger to her lips and shook her head, for she was both deaf and dumb. With a sinking heart, he continued his struggle downwards – for surely, he thought, he would find water at the bottom of the valley. The strange figure followed, and a deeper silence than ever closed in around them, but as they neared the bottom of the valley Sanfu heard a faint sound in the distance. He cupped his hand to his ear, and thought he could hear the mournful coo of a dove. "Where there is life," he decided, "there must be water." So he pressed on. The cooing became louder as they went on down, until finally he distinctly heard the words:

"My father is dead,
My mother is dead,
My brothers and sisters
are dead, dead, dead.
I sit here alone,
alone on my own.
My heart is throbbing,
throbbing, throbbing, throbbing!"

it moaned, the sad song that doves have lamented since the beginning of time. Still louder grew the cooing, until at last Sanfu and the silent figure were standing in a wide open space opposite an enormous jet-black rock that towered into the sky. On either side of him, sheer-sided red cliffs had suddenly appeared. At the bottom of the valley he saw a broad, black and sinister river. The cooing went on, becoming ever more melancholy. At the foot of the tall black rock he saw three caves, and at the entrance to the middle one sat a most beautiful white dove. It was she who was singing the mournful song. On either side of her stood a black raven. As soon as the ravens saw Sanfu, they began to dance faster and faster until, utterly exhausted, they collapsed at the dove's feet.

The white dove raised her head proudly to address Sanfu. "Welcome to our country, good Sanfu. For many years we have awaited your arrival."

Sanfu decided there must be magic here. How else could a talking dove be expecting him? So he asked, "How is it that you know my name and why should you await me?"

"The time has come;' answered the dove, "for you to do us a great service. We have awaited your arrival for as many days as there are stars in the sky. We are weary of our captivity."

"I am willing to help you," said Sanfu at once. "Tell me what I must do."

"Repeat these magic words after me three times;' the dove replied.

"River, river, magic river,
You bewitched us long ago;
Change us from the shapes you gave us
Back to the forms we used to know."

Three times Sanfu repeated the magic words. Immediately there was a loud creaking sound, and the cave on the right-hand side of the White Dove opened to a burst of singing from thousands of birds that had been imprisoned within. Birds of every size and colour now flashed before his admiring eyes, and beyond them were mountains and lakes, forests and flowers, beautiful beyond words. He gazed at the sight in astonishment as gradually

the huge cave closed again upon the birds. At the same time the raven on the right-hand side of the White Dove rose slowly to its feet, to gaze into the distance as though nothing had happened.

"Is this all I must do?" asked Sanfu; "and what does it mean?"

"This is only the beginning," replied the White Dove. "The birds you have seen are the lovely maidens of this valley, who were bewitched into birds long ago, and you must set them free. Now, repeat the magic words again three times."

Three times more Sanfu chanted the words, and immediately the cave on the left-hand side of the White Dove creaked open, revealing herd upon herd of every wild animal that he had ever seen, and many more besides. Their skins shone like satin, and the cries that came from them all but drowned the singing of the birds. They stood knee-deep in lush green pastures where sparkling streams reflected soft sunlight. Then this cave too, slowly closed its yawning entrance, while the second black raven rose slowly to its feet and, like its companion, gazed into the distance.

"Those;' said the White Dove, "are the warriors belonging to our king, my father. They, too, are under the spell of the big black river, and you have been chosen to set us free."

"There is a third cave," broke in Sanfu. "Tell me what it holds!"

"That I cannot tell you now," replied the White Dove. "It cannot be opened until you have been our guest for the passing of ten full moons. Stay with us, good Prince, for you alone can bring our imprisonment to an end."

"What about my own people, White Dove?" asked Sanfu with a sinking heart. "How can I tell them where I am? Otherwise they will think me dead."

"There is no way to tell them," replied the White Dove. "You must trust my word that your reward will be worth their sorrow. But listen – if you leave us before your service is completed, a most dreadful fate will befall you. You will become an enormous and fearsome spider – so terrible to look upon, that all living things will avoid you with horror, and your home will be in damp and dark places. Your life will be one of loneliness and sorrow. Think well on this matter, good Sanfu."

"Such a fate seems too terrible for me to refuse," replied Sanfu miserably. "I give you my word that I will stay, oh most beautiful of all doves."

"It is well," sighed the White Dove in a tone of relief. She turned to where the dumb woman stood behind her, took her staff from her and threw it to the ground. As the staff left the old woman's hand she vanished, though the two ravens fell with the staff, to remain motionless where they had fallen.

"You are both hungry and thirsty," said the dove and, with a nod of her head towards the staff, she ordered food and drink. These appeared at once – all that a hungry man could desire. Sanfu ate and drank until he was satisfied, then lay down and slept.

Never again did the White Dove speak; and never again did Sanfu see the two black ravens. Yet strangely, he never suffered from hunger or heat or cold, for food and drink appeared whenever he wished and the weather passed him by. It was a long and weary wait, but eventually the ten moons passed, and Sanfu stood before the White Dove, whom he had watched for all that time.

"I have not failed you," he said to her, "and the time for my release has come. What is there left for me to do?"

"Repeat the same magic words three times more," she replied, and again he said,

> "River, river, magic river,
> You bewitched us long ago;
> Change us from the shapes you gave us
> Back to the forms we used to know."

There was a sound of distant rumbling, and the third cave gradually opened, growing larger as it did so. The imprisoning valley faded away; the sluggish black river vanished; the rocks and boulders turned into beautiful glossy cattle, while the stones became sheep and goats which grazed peacefully amongst rich pastures. Crops stood ready for the reapers and all the countryside was smiling. Gone were the steep sinister cliffs and instead there stood before him the same twin peaks between which he had entered the valley those long ten months before.

"Now, twice more, good Sanfu – your task is nearly done," said the dove with longing.

As his voice ceased for the second time, the cave on the left-hand side of the dove burst open. Out flew flock upon flock of the beautiful birds that had been imprisoned there. Circling and dipping as they flew, their brilliant plumage flashed in the sun.

For the third time Sanfu repeated the magic words, and the door of the animal cave opened, to release the herds of joyful creatures that rushed headlong into the lovely valley that awaited them.

"Again, Sanfu, again!" cried the dove, in a frenzy of excitement, and for the fourth and last time he obeyed her.

Now came the most wonderful change of all, and he watched in astonishment as the birds took human shape, turning into hundreds upon hundreds of beautiful women and children, who surrounded the loveliest girl he had ever seen. They sang and danced for joy, rejoicing to use their human limbs once more. At the same time the herds of buck and animals became splendid warriors, who clashed their gleaming spears against their dappled ox-hide shields, as their ringed cat-tail aprons swung from their hips. A royal impi, with the proud pink beads on their necks and blood-red feathers fixed in their hair. At their head was their king, majestic and dignified in his leopard-skin trappings. On each side of the king strode a handsome prince – who had, for long years, stood as black ravens on either side of the White Dove at the entrance to the cave. The old woman herself was there, carrying the same tall staff, but now changed back into the tribe's trusted and wise Sangoma.

Shouts of gratitude rose for the man who had released them from the cruel spell, and from the centre of the crowd of women, there came towards him the lovely girl he had noticed a short while before. "At last you see me in my human form, good Sanfu," she said "for I am the White Dove!"

Then the king spoke: "Noble prince, we owe you so great a debt that anything you wish shall be yours; cattle, sheep, goats – up to half my kingdom!"

Sanfu looked down and did not answer.

"What?" exclaimed the king after a while; "do I not offer enough? Name your wish, and you shall have it."

"I have only one wish," replied Sanfu, at last raising his eyes, "and it is to marry the loveliest princess in the land – the White Dove. Cattle and sheep I do not need for my own father is also a king, who will give me all the wealth a son could desire. My marriage gifts to you will be as great as you desire, but you alone are able to give me what my heart longs for."

His eyes met those of the White Dove, who was now smiling happily at Sanfu's request.

"I see that my daughter already loves you," said the king, and he paused in thought. "I must consult the elders of our tribe. Have patience while we discuss the matter."

It was a long, long time that the king kept Sanfu waiting for his answer, for in all such matters of importance, the greater the prize, the longer the discussion, and it was a weary wait indeed. Sanfu was almost despairing when at last the day came when the king sent for him, and granted his request.

"I must make one condition though," the king ended, "and that is you become one of my tribe, and live with us for ever. For the White Dove is our dearest possession, and we cannot let her go. So hurry home, greet your family and return to us again. My blessings go with you."

Sanfu's parents had long thought that he was dead, killed by wild beasts. They welcomed him with great rejoicing and marvelled when he told his tale.

In due course his father sent him back with full honour, together with an impi of picked warriors, and a bridal-gift enough to satisfy any king.

Amongst the many festivities in "The Valley of the Birds" a magnificent marriage feast was held, and the love and happiness of the bride and her groom lasted to the end of their lives. The ageing king never regretted the reward that Sanfu had won. As his sons were now both ruling their own kingdoms in faraway lands, the old man was happy before he died to hand over the governing of his kingdom to Sanfu and the White Dove.

THE LION'S POOL

SWAZI

Thembekeli and her new husband spent the first year of their married life in the home of her mother-in-law. That was accepted as a wise custom, for there were many things that a young bride needs to learn from an older woman. The marriage had been expensive for her husband Vuka, because her father had demanded many fine, sleek cows for her wedding gift. However, he had no regrets, for she was a good wife. Not only was she good-looking and hard-working, but never had he known a better cook – and she took pride in providing the tastiest meals for his homecoming, when they returned together from their daily work in the fields. They grew beans and pumpkins besides the yearly supply of mealies, and Vuka's mother went with them on their daily trips for she, too, worked on her own patch of land.

From early morning to late afternoon the three hoed and weeded in their precious fields, to make sure of a good harvest to feed them in the winter. They returned to their home tired and hungry as the shadows lengthened. There Vuka always found the tastiest meal awaiting him, which his young wife had prepared in the early hours of the day, for she was anxious to show her husband how well she would cook and brew his favourite beer.

Thembekeli's mother-in-law was a greedy old woman who eyed her son's good food each day with increasing envy. She muttered to herself as she bent to her daily hoeing; there would be no tasty meal awaiting her, after her day's work was done. Admittedly she could rise early to cook herself a tasty evening meal, but somehow she never got round to it, for she liked to lie in bed as long as she could.

The more the old woman thought about it, the more greedy and jealous she became. Whatever happened, she must at least have a taste of her son's lovely evening meal, and she thought out a cunning plan. She took off her cow-skin apron and, digging her hoe firmly into the earth, draped the garment carefully over the handle. "Now," she ordered the hoe, "keep on digging until I return!" Obediently the hoe rose and fell, continuing her work.

Delighted with this trick, the old woman hurried home, knowing that if her son should look towards her field, he would see what appeared to be her figure, hard at work. "How very clever of me!" she chuckled as she hastened on her way.

"One tiny taste!" she thought as she scooped a handful of the tender mealies, spinach and pumpkin from her son's pot. "Salted just right too!" Then, as she sipped from the calabash that stood against the wall of the hut, "What excellent beer! The best in the land." It all tasted so delicious, that before long both the pot and the calabash were empty. She gave a belch of satisfaction and hurried back to her field. There was her hoe, with her apron still draped over the handle, working obediently as she had left it. It looked exactly like an old woman at work.

It had been a particularly hot and tiring day for Vuka and his wife, so they were glad when the shadows had lengthened sufficiently for them to shoulder their hoes and return to their cosy hut. They called to the old woman as they passed her field, and she joined Thembekeli in gathering wood for their evening fire as they went home. Vuka strode ahead, eager for his evening meal, but imagine his disappointment and surprise, when he found nothing but an empty pot and an empty calabash which did nothing to satisfy his hunger or thirst!

"Look at this!" he exclaimed to his wife as she entered the hut and put down her bundle of wood.

"A thief has been here while we worked, and has eaten our evening meal!" He went to his mother's hut to see if she, too, had been robbed.

"No," replied the old woman, with a look of pretended surprise on her face. "Everything is as I left it this morning."

On the following morning she played the same trick again, only this time the old woman dared to do even more. She put on her son's best jackal-skin cloak, dressed herself in the love-beads that had been so carefully made for him by his bride, took down the walking stick from its peg on the wall and, carrying the tasty meal into the sunshine, sat down to enjoy it. Once more it was not long before she had eaten the food and drunk the beer; but this time she had added insult to injury, for never never should a woman wear the clothes and ornaments of a man, nor eat her meal in the sunshine.

That evening when they returned, Vuka found the same disappointment waiting for him. "Tomorrow I will stay behind," he told Thembekeli, "and catch the thief as he enters our hut." But the old woman, guessing his plan, worked steadily at her crops all day, and so there was no thief for Vuka to catch.

"Tomorrow I will work in the fields again," he told his wife that night, "and later I shall return and hide behind a bush, for perhaps someone watches until we leave."

The three left for the fields after they had eaten next morning, and as the sun climbed high into the heavens Vuka slipped back to hide behind a bush that overlooked his hut. He was astonished when he saw his mother walk boldly into the hut, and appear soon after dressed in his best clothes, while in her hands she carried his own plate – full of food and the pot of beer. She sang gaily as she sat down outside the hut to enjoy her feast – but her song turned to moans of shame when her son came out from behind the bush and she knew she had been caught.

"How dare you do this? I should kill you!" he exclaimed angrily.

"Oh, my son, my son!" she wept, "I do deserve to be punished. Oh, whatever made me do this dreadful thing. My greed will be my downfall."

"I will spare your life," said Vuka, "but your greedy stomach needs a lesson. Take this," and he handed her an earthen pot, "and do not return until you have filled it with the clear and sparkling water from a pool in which no creature has ever lived. It will mean a long and dangerous journey, but only when it has been completed, will I forgive you."

With many tears the old woman put the pot on her shoulder and left upon her journey. For many days she wandered, searching, until eventually she reached a clear and sparkling pool, where water lilies and reeds grew at the water's edge. She stooped down hopefully. "Does anyone live in this pool?" she asked.

"Yes," croaked a chorus of frogs, appearing on the surface of the water and scrambling onto the lily leaves. "This is our home. Go away!" Sighing sadly, she rose to continue her search.

The night times were frightening, and she had little sleep when she heard the wild animals moving stealthily around her. More than once she heard a lion roar, and the mocking laugh of the hyena – which often carries a witch upon its back – added to her terror. Food was always scarce, for there were few roots and berries and her search for them took much of the day.

Further and further from her home she wandered, and the days passed into weeks. Many a new moon rose before she found another pool that raised her hopes. No reeds or water-lilies surrounded this one, and the blue sky and clouds above were all that were reflected in its quiet waters. "Surely," she said to herself, "nothing could have its home in such stillness." So she bent down hopefully. "Does anyone live in these quiet waters?" she asked, but her hopes were dashed when a shoal of fish raised their heads above the water and many voices mocked, "Yes, it is our home. Go away!"

She sat sadly at the water's edge for some time, and then rose once more to continue her search. The sun beat down mercilessly as she picked up her pot and trudged on. Again the days passed into weeks as the new moon rose and fell until, worn out with anguish and despair she saw the cool, inviting shade of a large forest ahead. At least, she thought, here she would find shelter from the cruel sun, and she stumbled into its gloom. She sat down to rest under the refreshing shade, only to feel some strange force calling her on. Tiny paths spread out in front of her, and many buck and small animals stopped to gaze.

She went further into the forest, drawn on by the same strange, compelling force, until at last she came to a large clearing. In the centre was a clear still pool, beside a tall tree. By now she needed water for her parched throat, and she stooped to drink. The reflection of her tired and worn face brought back the memory of her search, and she wearily called into the silent depths, "Does anyone live in this quiet pool?" There was no reply, so she asked the question again. Once more there was silence. Her thirst forgotten, she was about to dip her pot into the water when angry voices behind her said, "Woman, what do you want? Do you know whose kingdom you are in? This is the Lion's Pool."

She looked round fearfully, to see a group of animals had gathered threateningly behind her.

"Please," she faltered, "do not hurt me. I want only to quench my thirst and fill my pot from your silent pool. When this is done, I will return home, leaving my blessings with you."

"You are fortunate," said one, "that our lord the lion is not here for he would kill you for your daring. However, we will have pity upon you, for you appear to be in need of our help."

The old woman thanked them and gratefully drank as the animals watched. Then, dipping the pot into the sparkling water, she filled it. But when she tried to rise she found that the roots of the tree had grown over her legs, binding her securely to the ground. She burst into tears, and cried out, "Dear animals, please help me!"

They muttered together, and at last she heard one say, "We must guard her against the Lion's anger, for the spell said that one day a human would set us free. Giraffe, you must be on guard. With your long neck you can watch through the tree tops and see him coming."

"No, no," replied the giraffe, "for I can't see in the dark, and our lord lion often returns at night.

Surely the leopard would make a better guard?" But the leopard too refused, pointing out that, although he could see in the dark, it was in the night time that he hunted his food and if he got too hungry, he might be tempted to eat her.

It was then that the hare stepped forward. He was always looked up to for his wisdom. "Let me use my sharp teeth," he said, "to gnaw through roots that bind her. Perhaps she will be of more use to us alive than dead, and she has done us no harm."

They nodded in agreement, and the hare at once began the long task he had chosen, until finally he had gnawed through the last root, and the woman rose thankfully to her feet. She praised the hare for his help and the other animals for their kindness, filled her pot from the pool and left the forest as fast as her legs would take her.·

Many weeks later she reached her home, but she had travelled swiftly and with a light heart. Food and water too, seemed less difficult to find, and she slept more peacefully at night, where all was quiet and at rest. "My son," she said when she arrived, "thanks to the kindness of some forest animals, my punishment has been completed. Here is the water from a pool in which no creature has ever lived."

As she handed the water to her son, a tremendous change was taking place in the forest of the Lion's Pool. The animals were changed into human beings, with the lion as their king; the trees became beautiful huts, and the many tracks became pathways round the kraal. They all sang the praises of the human who had released them from an age-old spell cast upon them by a wicked ogre, to be broken only when water from their magic pool was handed to the eldest son of an old woman.

When she had told him of her long and difficult journey, and of the kindness of the forest animals, Vuka was happy to forgive his mother for her wicked greed. As the years passed, he drew many people to live under the rule of his justice and protection, so that eventually he became the chief of a large and happy tribe.

THE TORTOISE
AND THE BIRDS

SWAZI

Long, long ago, besides the animals of the earth and birds of the air, there lived strange creatures whose home was far above the clouds. They were good and kind, and although it was only the birds who had ever seen them, the animals knew they were there. But no one knew their name.

One year there was drought everywhere and both birds and beasts were nearly dead from hunger. The Cloud People looked down in pity upon the earth dwellers and said, "Come up, all you who have wings, and let us feed you, for here there is plenty to eat."

The birds were delighted, and the news went from bird to bird that they should gather upon a certain big rock. They would fly up together from there. While they were waiting for the late arrivals they twittered excitedly about the feast awaiting them. In this rock were many hollows and holes, and in one of them lived two tortoises. They, too, were suffering from hunger, and while his wife was away hunting for a morsel of food, her husband listened to the excited chattering of the birds.

"Oh, I wish I had wings like you, my friends!" he said, coming out of his hole to join them.

"Can't you take me with you? I'm just as hungry as you are." Of course, he realised, he did not look like a bird, but since the invitation had included all the creatures that could fly, the Cloud People would surely take pity on him too.

"We'd be happy to have you with us," answered the birds, "but you are too heavy for us to carry, and you can't fly without wings."

"Oh, but I'm starving!" he sobbed. They listened to him with sympathy, and discussed the matter among themselves.

"Couldn't we each pluck a feather from our wings, and fix them to his feet?" they wondered. This was an exciting idea. Then, when they arrived above the clouds, they could proudly present the tortoise as their king. Without delay they set to work, and it was a strange looking creature that at last took to the air surrounded by his feathered friends.

The birds couldn't help laughing because he looked so funny, but their plan succeeded and the tortoise soared into the sky with them.

"What shall we call him?" the birds asked one another as they neared the home of their cloud friends. Many names were suggested, and they finally decided that he should be called

"All Of You", meaning that he was to represent all of them – the greatest of them all. So when they arrived, he was introduced as King All Of You.

The Cloud People were very honoured to think that the birds had brought their king to visit them, and at once prepared a great feast. "Whose food is this?" asked the birds politely, as they were taken into the hut where all the fine dishes were spread out.

"It is for 'all of you'," replied the Cloud People. The tortoise, hearing his new name called out strode forward and, with great relish ate nearly all the food that had been provided, leaving very little indeed for his companions.

"It must be their custom," thought the Cloud People, "to see that their king satisfies his wants, before they eat themselves." So they stood aside while the tortoise enjoyed all the food within his reach.

The birds were so angry at the tortoise's greed, that after they had picked up the few scraps of food that were left, they took back all the feathers they had so carefully attached to his feet. Now he had no way to return to earth. Although it was no more than he deserved, he was weeping and wailing when the birds flew away, leaving him to his fate.

The parrot was the last to leave. "Please, friend parrot," begged the unfortunate tortoise, "have pity upon me. Please go at once to my wife and tell her to gather all the soft grass that she can find, and to pile it high near the big rock, so that I can land on it safely, for otherwise I shall be killed."

However, the parrot was as hungry as the other birds, so he, too, was angry. The message he took to the tortoise's wife was that her husband wished her to gather as many rocks and stones as she was able, and to build them into a platform, on which he would land.

This the wife duly did, and down jumped the tortoise. What a crash-landing! His nice smooth shell was broken into many pieces, and although his wife nursed him devotedly, the scars left between his bits of broken shell never left him. They have shown to this very day on all tortoises ever since – a reminder of the day when he jumped from the clouds.

Narrator: Joyce D. Khumalo

HALF CHILD

SWAZI

" I must consult a 'Wise One', a Sangoma, to learn why, of all the women in the kraal, you alone, have no children," said a husband to his childless wife. So he went to a woman in a neighbouring village who was well known for her wisdom.

"Bring me a sleek young beast from your herd, for I shall use its fat in the medicine needed for your wife," she said. But, besides being bad tempered, the man was mean, so he chose a hornless beast without a tail, and drove it to the old woman on the following morning.

"Your punishment for bringing me this imperfect beast," said the Sangoma, "will be that you will have a son without arms or legs; but I warn you to tell no one of this matter. Return now to your wife, and remember my words."

In spite of her fame, the husband did not believe the old woman's threat, and told all his friends the result of his visit – but his wife he did not tell. As a result, when she knew that a child was on its way, the woman's heart was filled with gladness. Her joy soon turned to sorrow, however, for the girl-baby was not welcomed by her husband. "I paid for a son," he said angrily. "I will not have her. Take the child away."

The poor woman pleaded with her husband to be allowed to keep her baby daughter, but when she was three years old the cruel father made her take the child into the wilds, to be devoured by hyenas. The creatures of the wild, however, proved kinder than her human father, for they did not touch her.

She grew up under the shelter of the overhanging rock under which her mother had left her. Her food was the honey that trickled down the rock from a bees' nest overhead, and she gathered the berries and roots that grew around her little home. Sometimes, too, her mother left food for her as she went to hoe her lands. In her loneliness the child grew more beautiful as the years passed, and she learned many secrets of the wilds.

After the birth of the baby girl, the husband returned to the Sangoma, to complain that he had paid for a son, and he therefore refused to accept the daughter. He was angry that his wife had failed him once again.

"Did I not warn you to be silent?" the old woman reminded him. "You shall have your son!" The days went by, and once more his wife knew that a baby was to be born to her. This time it was a son, but the old woman's warning proved only too true, for he had neither arms nor legs. They called him Half Child, and, although it was a great grief to the poor mother, she loved him even more for what he was. As she could get no one to look after him by day, she was forced to leave him locked in her hut while she and her husband attended to the farming.

One day his sister came in secretly from her hiding-place. She found her mother's hut and called out, "Let me in, Half Child. I am your sister, who was sent by our hard-hearted father to live in the wilds. Let me in."

"How can I let you in, when I have no arms or legs?" asked the boy, so the girl opened the door. "Half Child," she said, "have arms and legs!" and arms and legs immediately appeared upon the boy.

"Now I will do our mother's work for her," said the girl. She swept the hut, fetched water from the spring, and cooked a tasty meal for their parents' return. "Don't tell anybody that I have been here," she told him. "If your mother asks who has done the work, tell her that you did it. Now, brother Half Child, arms and legs, depart!" Immediately he was once more as helpless as before, without either arms or legs. The girl then hurried back to her home under the overhanging rock.

The mother and father were astonished on their return from the fields, to find all that had been done at home while they were out. "Who has done all this?" asked the mother.

"I did it," the boy replied.

"Then, let me see you do it," she told him.

"I don't do something twice," was all that he answered, and his mother was left wondering. Every day after that, the sister came to do the housework, saying as she opened the door, "Half Child, arms and legs, appear!" and as she left, "Half Child, arms and legs, depart!" Every time her magic order was obeyed.

One day, when she needed water for cooking the evening meal, the girl told Half Child to fetch it from the spring. But once the boy felt the soft green grass under his feet he ran, and ran and ran; far beyond the spring and up the hill beyond. She called for him to come back, but he ran on and on, until finally she cried out, "Half Child, arms and legs, depart!" At once the boy fell to the path, as helpless as before.

On her way home that evening, the mother found her son lying exactly where he had fallen.

"How did you get here?" she asked in surprise.

"I came by myself," he replied.

"Well, let me see you go home again," she demanded.

"I don't do something twice," he answered stubbornly. So without arguing she picked him up and, putting him on her back, continued along the path.

Now, on this very day her husband had decided to remain in hiding at home to discover the reason for such strange happenings in their hut and, having witnessed all that had taken place, caught the girl as she was about to return to her rock shelter.

"She is too beautiful to escape me before I find out where she comes from," he thought to himself.

In answer, she told him of her lonely life since he had sent her into the wilds as a small child. Thinking of the fine cows he would add to his herd in exchange for such a lovely daughter, he now told her that she must come and live in her proper home. To this the girl readily agreed.

Soon they saw the mother in the distance, carrying Half Child on her back. "Half Child, arms and legs, appear!" called out his sister, and immediately the boy jumped from his mother's back, and ran along the path in front of her, singing and laughing, and leaping for joy.

The mother was astonished at the sudden change in her helpless son, but her astonishment was even greater when she reached her hut, to find her husband and daughter awaiting her arrival. With joy and surprise, she found that her husband was now willing to accept the daughter he had so cruelly driven into the wilds for the hyenas to devour, so many years ago.

The husband needless to say, was also pleased for, apart from now having a son with arms and legs, he had a marriageable daughter who would not only increase his wealth, but who had also, through her life of solitude, learned the art of magic.

Not very long after this, the sister and a party of girls from nearby went to gather red clay, with which to beautify themselves. Half Child decided to follow them, but his sister told him that this was work for girls alone, and bade him to go home. They had nearly reached the clay-pit when they looked back and saw that the boy was still following.

The sister was angry and returned to beat him, saying as she did so, "Half Child, arms and legs, depart!" which left the boy helpless on the path. "It serves him right," she said to her companions, "for disobeying me."

They had just finished filling their pots with clay, when a violent storm broke, beating down mercilessly upon their unprotected bodies. "Your brother!" exclaimed the girls. "We must hurry back for he is helpless!"

Running through the rain to where he lay, they found to their surprise, that the boy was laughing, with dry earth all around him. "Sister," he said, "you beat me, which made me angry, but I forgive you. Look, no rain has touched me. Come close to me, all of you, and you can shelter from the storm."

The girls did, and while the rain continued to pour down everywhere else, not a single drop fell where they were gathered around the boy. His sister, sorry for the beating she had given him, quickly restored his limbs and, to the astonishment of them all, he said, "My father's hut, come here!" and immediately his father's hut covered them. Then he added, "My father and mother, with their all possessions, come here!" and at once this happened too, so they all took refuge until the storm had passed.

The father and mother never returned to the old kraal, but started a little community of their own, where they lived happily for ever after. And his sister never took Half Child's arms and legs away again – for now he had found a magic more powerful even than her own.

UMUSHA MWAICE
THE LITTLE
SLAVE GIRL

ZAMBIA

Long, long ago there lived a chief who had three wives. Two of these wives had large families, many sons and six daughters between them. The third wife, however, was childless, and the other two laughed her to scorn.

The six daughters were a comfort to their mothers in all their daily tasks, helping them to gather wood and water, and to work in the fields. But not one of them would raise a finger to help the childless woman, and life was hard and lonely for her.

One day, while she was fetching water from the river, this sad woman burst into tears and cried out, "Why is it that I have no daughter to help me with my work? Where, oh where, can I get one?"

Akakantote, the praying mantis, bringer of goodness and mercy, was nearby and heard her cries. The little insect answered, "If you are able to cure my troubles, I will help you in return." He then showed the woman an ugly festering sore on his body.

The childless wife was kind at heart, so she picked up the little mantis and sucked the poison from his sore, saying, "I am happy to do far more than this for you, if you want me to." And the magic of her lips healed Akakantote's sore.

The mantis was very grateful to the woman for the help she had given him, and said in gratitude, "You have healed me of a painful sore; my reward for your kindness will be the daughter you desire."

The little insect handed her a stick, saying, "Take this stick, and keep it hidden from sight. Put it in a clay pot in the corner of your hut, and leave it for three days and nights."

The woman thanked Akakantote, and when she had drawn water from the river, she returned to her hut, where she did as the insect had told her.

There was a great deal of rude laughter when the lonely woman mentioned the kindness of the mantis, and the second wife jeered at her so much that the chief became very angry, and banished this hard-mouthed wife from his village. He comforted the childless one, and said, "Do not let the hard words of these two hurt you, for you, too, are my wife, and I do not blame you that you are childless."

Now, the two cruel wives were very fond of each other, so the first wife took the children of the banished one and cared for them as her own.

When three days had gone by and there was no sign of Akakantote's promise coming true, the woman was deeply disappointed and felt that her hopes had been raised for nothing. But she was wrong, because one day she did find a lovely baby girl where the stick had been, and her joy was beyond words.

When the chief's first wife saw the beautiful baby, she was so jealous that she refused to believe the story of the mantis, and accused the woman of stealing the baby. After that, the first wife grew more and more cruel and unkind to the little one's mother, until eventually she killed the poor woman. The chief was saddened by his wife's death, though he did not know how it had happened. Since his dead wife had owned a fine cow, he gave it to her new-born child. The cow was said to be magic, but no one knew how.

As she grew up, the child cried for the missing love of her dead mother. But the more she cried, the more her step-mother beat and ill-used her, calling her Umusha Mwaice the "Little Slave", and making her do all the menial work that was usually given to the slaves in the royal kraal. She was also at the mercy of the six royal half-sisters, who made her mend their bead-work and sew their cloth. She was indeed their "little slave", and she knew nothing else in the years while she was growing up.

Now, in a neighbouring country there lived a wealthy and highly respected chief, whose son had at this time reached the age of marriage. This mighty chief sent word to the father of the seven girls to say that he wished his noble son to choose a bride from among his neighbour's many daughters. "The honour that I do to your kingdom is great," he said, "so it would be wise to make suitable preparations to receive my heir."

All was bustle and hurry in the royal kraal, each sister being anxious to outdo the other five in hopes of catching the prince's eye. Each begged her father to buy her beads and finery in preparation for the great day.

But the youngest one asked for nothing, as she had not been included in the celebrations, and never imagined that any important visitor would look at her. However, before he went to the market to buy what was needed, the father called Little Slave to him and asked, "When I am buying the best for your six half-sisters, what shall I get for you?"

"Father," she answered, "if a little stick should fall upon your path as you travel through the forest, please bring it to me. That's all I want."

The chief left with his seven daughters' requests, and brought back from his journey many beautiful gifts for the six proud ones – but he bought nothing for the youngest one. But as he passed through the forest on his way home though, a twig fell from a tree and landed on the path. Remembering what Little Slave had asked, he picked it up, and kept it for her.

The six sisters laughed as Little Slave took her gift and clasping it in her hand, stole away to her mother's grave. She cried as she planted the stick and, as she watched in wonder, she saw it grow before her eyes into a graceful tree. Added to this, her mother came alive out of the grave and said, "Don't weep, my daughter. Tell me what I must do for you!"

In between her tears, Little Slave told her mother her long, sad tale. Then the woman gathered dew from the magic tree, and in it she bathed her daughter, who at once became more beautiful even than she had been before. The magic leaves turned to clothes far, far finer than those which her six wicked half-sisters wore; and when her mother had dressed her in them, she sent the child to the royal kraal.

Her step-mother, however, was so angry when she saw the loveliness of the magic clothes, that she beat Little Slave and complained, "Where did you steal such lovely clothes? They are far too good for such as you." So she pulled them off the child, and gave them to one of her own daughters, while she sent Little Slave back to her tasks of smearing the royal floors with mud, pounding casava flour, and doing the slaves' jobs as before.

When her tasks had been done, Little Slave went back to her mother's grave and, as she wept beside it, her mother appeared once more. "Go," said the woman, "and find the magic cow, which once was mine. Ask her to swallow you." The girl knew the cow well, for she had cared for it, as her own, and it now obediently did as it was told and swallowed Little Slave. Inside the cow, her slave's clothes were changed to purest silk – more beautiful even than those that she had worn before. Then out of the cow's mouth she came again and went to the royal kraal.

This time the step-mother was angrier than ever, and when she heard that the clothes had come out of the stomach of the magic cow, she killed the cow, and invited all the people of the kraal to share her feast of its meat. Umusha Mwaice was too sad to join in. Instead when the feast was over, she gathered up the bones.

"Aha," jeered the step-mother, "she would not eat the meat, but now she picks the bones!" Little Slave took no notice. She carried the bones to the river and threw them far out into the

35

water. Immediately there appeared on the river bank, some large and splendid huts, more magnificent than those of the royal kraal, and in them were all things needed for a bride, and food for all.

"Whose huts are those?" asked the step-mother.

"They must belong to the one who owned the cow!" replied the people of the kraal.

At this she screamed with rage, "Then I will kill her as well!" She took Little Slave into the royal kitchen, dug a hole under the cooking stones, and there she buried the girl alive.

As it happened, that was the very day that the son of the great chief came to choose his bride. In the royal kitchen all was bustle and excitement as the cooks prepared a feast for the honoured guest. "Ah!" chuckled the step-mother, very pleased with herself, "soon our royal visitor will make his choice and it will have to be one of these six daughters, for who else is there for him to choose?"

During the morning, people wondered where Little Slave had gone. But as anyone who mentioned her name was made to do her work, nobody said anything more.

Dressed in their best, the six sisters were brought one by one before the royal visitor for him to choose his future bride. But he liked none of them. "No," he said, shaking his head. "These are not for me. But tell me," he asked, "who owns those huts?" and he pointed to the beautiful huts on the river bank among the reeds and water. "Find her, and she shall be my bride."

Everyone searched in vain for the little slave girl, when suddenly the cock began to crow, "The owner of those huts is ... " but he did not finish the sentence because the step-mother interrupted loudly, "I will kill that cock!"

"Do not let her," cried the people, because they wanted to hear what else the cock had to say.

But the cock would not be silenced. He crowed again, "The owner of those huts is buried under the ..." The chief's wife caught the cock by the neck, and began to strangle him, but not quite in time. He managed to gasp out the last words, " . . . the cooking stones."

At once the search began. From kitchen to kitchen the people rushed, digging under the cooking stones, until at last they reached the kitchen of the royal huts and there, in the hole under the cooking stones, they found Little Slave. When they had revived and comforted her, they led her to the son of the noble chief and his eyes shone with happiness. Addressing his chief councillor he said, "Hurry to our country with this message to my father. Tell him that I have found the bride of my heart, and I beg him to prepare the feast of all feasts to welcome her to her future home."

Umusha Mwaice's father then gave orders for feasting and celebrations of equal magnificence to take place throughout his kingdom. So, when all those preparations had been completed, in joy and splendour, the noble chief's son married the little slave girl, while the six cruel half-sisters hung their heads in jealousy and anger.

THE MAGIC ANTHILL

ZAMBIA

In a faraway village in the heart of Africa, there lived a girl more beautiful than any in the land. All men wanted her as their bride, but one by one she turned them away, saying scornfully to her father, "What! Do you think I could be satisfied with such as that?" In that way many months and years passed by.

But one day, as she and her young brother sat talking on the river bank where she had gone to draw water, a particularly handsome man approached them. "Beautiful one," he said to the girl, "will you guide me to your father's home? I am ill, and I need shelter in his hut for a while."

"What strong arms!" she thought to herself. "What flashing eyes! What strength! This must be the husband I have been waiting for!" But all she said to him, in a rather off-hand way was, "My brother will guide you to my father's kraal, for I'm waiting for someone else." This was not the truth, but she decided to make him feel that she had other interests.

Her brother was only too happy to help, because he was just as impressed by the young man's looks. On arrival at the kraal the stranger was kindly received, and offered shelter until he was well again.

As the days went by, the young man made no attempt to leave, and the girl did her best to capture the handsome and fascinating stranger. The stranger, on his part, made himself so useful to everyone that the girl's father was delighted when he asked for the hand of his lovely daughter. So the two were married.

With the bridegroom now living at the home of his bride, everyone was amazed at his success as a hunter. Whenever he went out in search of meat, he brought back a buck, while the other villagers usually returned empty-handed.

Now, this intrigued the girl's young brother, and his respect for his new relative continued to grow until he decided, one day, to follow at a distance, to see how this clever brother-in-law had such success. If only he could learn such skill, his fame would spread throughout the land! His heart filled with excitement at the thought.

So, at the first opportunity, the boy crept after his brother-in-law. He saw him climb a large anthill, and heard him say in a loud voice, "Anthill, anthill, let us go and kill. My father-in-law wants meat!"

As the words left his lips, the handsome stranger changed into an enormous lion, and the magic anthill, with him crouched upon it, moved silently into a herd of buck that was grazing close at hand. With a savage roar and a mighty spring, the lion dragged the nearest buck to the ground, where he killed it.

The younger brother watched all this in astonishment and fear. Then, crouching out of sight, he ran quickly back to his father's kraal.

The boy hurried to his sister's hut and said to her, "Your husband is a 'Lion-man'. I saw him change his shape and kill a buck, as I was following him"

This made the sister very angry. She gave him a good beating and said, "You lie. He is a human being, just as you are." Not wanting to risk another beating, the boy remained silent.

After some months, the husband told his father-in-law that he wished to take his wife to his own home, so the two departed upon their long journey. The young brother longed to go with them but his sister said he told lies, so he was left behind.

However, he decided to follow them secretly, and it was not until they had reached the husband's home that they discovered the boy was there. The sister then relented, and they made him welcome. All went well for many days, and the husband regularly brought home from the hunt all the meat that they could eat.

The time came, though, when the boy awoke one night, to see an enormous lion standing over his sister, and heard it say in a gruff voice, "All the meat I have killed for you has made you nice and fat. You refused to marry any of your own people but, not knowing who I was, you married me. Now I am going to eat you!" He bared his great white fangs and prepared to seize her by the throat.

In fear the brother jumped up, and this broke the spell. The husband, turned to human shape once more, said, "Why do you not sleep, brother?"

"It is nothing," answered the boy. "There's a stone in my bed keeping me awake." Unable to carry out his plan, the husband lay down to sleep, thinking the boy had not seen him in his lion's form.

This happened several more times on the nights that followed, but the boy was on the watch, and each time he stopped the lion-man as he was about to kill the girl, until finally the boy told her what he had seen. Again his sister accused him of telling lies, and beat him as before, so he decided upon a plan which he hoped would save them both. After she had gone to sleep that night, he tied a string to one of her fingers and, holding the other end, he settled down to watch.

Presently he saw the lion-man creep into the hut and, bending over the girl, again take the form of a fearsome lion. He heard him say, "This time I shall eat you."

The brother gently pulled the string and, seeing the lion crouching over her as she woke, the girl called out, "Brother, brother, save me!"

Immediately the spell was broken and her husband, once more back in his human form, said soothingly, "What disturbs you, my beautiful? You are only dreaming. Go back to sleep." Once again, she stayed alive.

"Now," said the boy to his sister next morning, after the husband had gone upon his usual hunt, "was I speaking the truth?"

"You were indeed," replied the girl sorrowfully. "If only I had believed you. Now we are both likely to be eaten, for we're too far away from home for anyone to help."

"Quickly," said the boy, "follow me, for still there is a chance." He led her to an anthill nearby and, climbing onto it he pulled her after him, calling out as he did so, "Anthill, anthill, take us to our home." Obeying the magic words, the anthill rose up into the air, and swiftly carried them home.

The lion-man returned from his hunt just in time to see the anthill carry his prey over the treetops towards their home, and his mighty roar of rage shook the forest. With the spell of his magic anthill broken, he had to return to his lion form for ever more.

From that time onward, the lion-man roamed through the forest, afraid to seek his beautiful human wife at her father's home, for everyone would recognise him and kill him. He therefore made himself a promise to seek and kill all human beings that came his way.

Still today, people in Northern Zambia will say of a stranger, "Ask him about his home and his family, or you may find yourself marrying a lion."

THE SONG OF THE GOLDEN BIRDS

ZAMBIA

Once upon a time there lived a powerful chief who ruled over a wild country, far away from civilization. There were hard times for his people. Few traders came that way, and cloth for clothes became scarce. Eventually times grew so bad that no cloth had been available for many, many months, and the people's nakedness brought them deep sorrow and shame.

One day a large flight of Golden Birds, that shone like the rising sun, passed over the royal kraal and, as they flew singing overhead, they dropped a cloud of feathers, which formed into cloth as they floated to the ground – enough to clothe all the chief's many subjects.

Needless to say, there was rejoicing throughout the kingdom. Such a gift had never come to them before, and they marvelled at the kindness of the Golden Birds. However, as time passed, the cloth wore out and once again the people were all but naked.

Their chief therefore decided to send his eleven sons to look for the Golden Birds, so he called them to him. "Sons," he said, "go and search far and wide for the Golden Birds, and bring them back to me so that we can keep them here and have enough cloth for ever. Do not come back to me without them for, although you are my sons, I will kill you if you do."

The eleven sons at once prepared food for the journey, and departed on their travels.

Day after day they searched for the Golden Birds through the forests near and far, but nowhere did they find, or even hear of them. After many months they reached a village where, tired and footsore, the eldest of the eleven said, "Brothers, let us stay here for ever. We cannot return to our own country, for our father promised to kill us if we did so without carrying out his command."

He therefore looked for a wife, found one, and settled down to the local village life. The ten remaining brothers, however, continued upon their way, searching the countryside until they came to another village. Here the eldest of the remaining ten said the same as his elder brother had said, and he too stayed behind. He married one of the village maidens, while the remaining nine brothers went on without him.

The same thing happened again and again until at last there was only one brother left, the youngest of them all. This brother was now a man, for his search had lasted many years, and his journey had taken him far from home. One day, while passing through a forest he met Akakantote, the praying mantis, and the little insect said to him, "What brings you, a stranger, to our land?"

The youngest son told the mantis the story of his search for the Golden Birds. The mantis listened with interest and said, "You have become a man during your search, and you are still trying to obey your father's wish. Because of this, I will help you."

The mantis then took a small gourd, which he filled with flies and beads. He put a lid on it and gave it to the young man, saying, "This will lead you to your journey's end."

As the young man took the gourd into his hands, the flies and beads turned into the loathsome disease of scabies, which immediately spread all over his body. One fly only escaped from the gourd, and darted ahead of him. So, holding the gourd he followed the fly on and on.

After covering a long distance the little insect took him to a city where the people had such houses as he had never seen before, and where they had paler skins than he had ever seen. Here they caught and beat him, for the sight of a black man was strange to them, and the sores that covered his body disgusted them.

"What do you want?" they asked him.

"I am looking for the Golden Birds," he said. Just then there was a burst of song from the very birds themselves, and their golden brightness lit the sky as they passed above. He cried aloud for joy, for he thought he had reached his journey's end.

But the people said, "Who are you, so dirty and full of sores, that you come to our city and ask for our Golden Birds? We will let them go on one condition only. Many days' journey from here you will come to another, larger city, and there you will find a Magic Drum. Bring us the drum, and you may have our Golden Birds."

On he went again, still following the fly, and after many days travelling he reached the city of the Drum. Here he found that the houses were even stranger than the last, and the people paler skinned. Here they beat him more severely than before, and asked what he was looking for.

When they heard that he wanted their Magic Drum, they laughed loudly at his daring and said, "Bring us the Golden Queen from the City that rules over all the land. Then, and then only, may you have our Magic Drum."

Again he continued upon his travels, with the fly still leading the way, and it was many days later that he reached the greatest city of all. Once more he was caught and beaten more cruelly than ever, after which he was dragged before their ruler.

When this great man heard the story of his courage, from the time he set out upon his quest, and the difficulties that had come his way, he marvelled at the young man's determination – so much so, that he decided he would give him their precious Golden Queen who shone like the sun, as a reward for his bravery – and this he did. However, there was deep sorrow among the people, when, after he had rested, the youngest son left the city with their Queen.

Now that his search was ended, the little fly that had led him went back into the gourd which he still carried, and the disease that it had brought to him disappeared. Accompanied by the Golden Queen he began his journey back to the city of the Magic Drum, where he gave her to its people. But they were deeply ashamed at the way in which they had treated him when they had heard the story of his determination and courage, and of the trouble that had followed him since he left his home. They decided not to take the Golden Queen who shone like the sun, but to make him a present of the Magic Drum. So he left this city, taking with him the wonderful Drum as well as the beautiful Queen, and continued on his way to the city of the Golden Birds. There he gave the Drum to its people, in exchange for the Golden Birds.

However, the same thing happened again. They too were deeply ashamed of their cruelty, and gave him the Golden Birds saying, "Go, with our blessings and our birds, but we will not take the Magic Drum."

That was how it happened that the youngest son now possessed the Golden Queen who shone like the sun, the Magic Drum, and the Golden Birds. Not surprisingly, he married the beautiful Queen, while the Golden Birds sang, and the Magic Drum played, as they left the city on their long journey to his father's home.

On his way back, he met Akakantote the praying mantis once again. He told the mantis about his journey and its success. Then he returned the little gourd containing the flies and beads, thanking Akakantote for his kindness.

"It is nothing," the mantis assured him. "May you travel safely."

Now it happened that the Queen, when she left her home, was followed by her little dog. When they reached the village where the second youngest of the eleven brothers was living, they found that all was far from well. The youngest son found his brother dirty, sick, and very poor. The wife he had married had grown tired of him and no longer bothered to cook food. His brother comforted, clothed and fed him, and advised him to return to their father. So they went on together.

As he revisited all the places along his travels, the youngest son found first one brother and then the next, sick and nearly starving. One by one he comforted and cared for them, inviting them to join him and to leave their faithless wives behind.

Eventually the travellers drew near to their father's home. However, the unsuccessful brothers had become jealous, and the night before they were due to arrive, the eldest said to the other nine, "Let us kill our youngest brother. All praise and honour is bound to come to him. What will there be for us?"

At first the others refused, and said, "He has rescued us all. How can we think of harming him?"

In the end the eldest brother persuaded them by saying, "He will be our father's favourite, and that will be as good as death for us."

That was why, when they were nearing home the next morning, the ten elder brothers took him behind an anthill and strangled him. After a while, they told his Queen that he had been bitten by a snake, and was dead. As she wept over her husband's body, the Queen ceased to shine like the sun, the Magic Drum left off playing, and the Golden Birds stopped singing and were silent.

At this, the elder brother shrugged his shoulders and said to the Queen, "What does it matter? I will marry you instead."

During this time the Queen's little dog refused to leave the body of its dead master, and stayed on guard by his side, while the rest of the party continued their journey to his father's village.

When they arrived, the Queen was pale and still crying, the Drum was silent, and the birds no longer sang. When the eldest son said to the father, "Here are the Golden Birds you told us to bring to you," the chief answered, "These are not the birds I asked for. Where is their song? Where is their cloth? And who is this woman?"

The eldest son replied, "She is my wife."

"Where is my youngest son?" asked the chief.

When the brothers told the old man that his youngest son was dead, he was quite overcome and wept bitterly.

Meanwhile, when the little dog found that his master would not move, he licked his face and breathed into his nostrils. This succeeded in bringing life back into his body. Soon the man had recovered and he and the little dog followed the others into the father's village.

As the two drew near to the great gathering at the chief's hut, the Queen began, once more, to shine like the sun, the Magic Drum began to play, and the Golden Birds burst into song. The chief and his people were astonished. Then they saw the youngest son, whom they had been told was dead.

The ten brothers were afraid, for they knew that their father would now hear the truth. "He'll kill us," they whispered to each other.

The youngest son greeted his father warmly and gave him the many treasures that he had brought with him. Then he asked for all the people to be gathered together to hear his tale. He told them everything, from the beginning to the end and, when he had finished, the old chief was so angry that he sentenced his ten sons to death. After that, he called his youngest son to him and said, "My son, I have grown old while you were away, and it is my wish that you should take my place. You are now chief."

Amid great splendour and celebrations, the young chief was proclaimed ruler by all the old chiefs' subjects. His first act was to forgive his ten brothers, and to change their punishment to banishment from his kingdom for life. From that day until his death the Golden Birds supplied all the clothes they needed and delighted all around them with their song; the Magic Drum played; and the beautiful Golden Queen shone with love for him. With his dearly loved Queen, the youngest son lived a long and happy life, famed for his goodness, and ruling wisely and well until the end of his days.

"LOOK N'GAI, NO FISHES!"

KIKUYU

The Kikuyu People believe that in the days of long, long ago, when the Good Lord N'gai made his plans for all the creatures upon his earth, he made the hippopotamus as an animal of the forests and plains. But the hippopotamus was greedy and, finding plenty of food all round him and no enemies to worry about, he grew fatter, and fatter and fatter. And the fatter he grew, the more he suffered from the heat of the Equatorial midday sun.

Day after day, when he waddled down to the river for his drink, he gazed with envy at the little fishes that swam in the pool which was cooled by the melted snows from far-away Mount Kenya. "Oh!" he would sigh, "how wonderful it would be if I could live, like N'gai's little fishes, in the clear, cool, refreshing water!"

The hippopotamus pondered over his trouble for many days, and eventually decided to approach The Lord of All Creation. "Please, Good Lord N'gai," he cried loudly to the heavens upon one particularly hot day, "allow me to leave the forests and the plains. Let me live instead in the clear, cool waters of your rivers and lakes, for the heat of the fiery sun is killing me!"

"No," replied Lord N'gai, "for my little fishes are very dear to me, and if you were to live in the rivers and lakes, you might try a change of your eating habits, and begin to eat those little fishes. That would never do. No, you must continue to live upon the dry land."

So the hippopotamus stayed sadly in his home in the forests and plains, where the sun continued to beat down mercilessly on his unprotected hide. "This is more than I can bear!" moaned the poor creature. "Please, please, Good Lord N'gai, let me leave the forests and plains, and become a creature of the rivers and lakes. I promise most faithfully that I will not eat your little fishes."

The Great Lord N'gai thought the matter over, while he looked down upon the plains baking in the heat of the tropical sun, and eventually his heart softened. "Very well," he agreed, "I will allow you to live in my rivers and lakes, but how will you prove to me that you are not eating my little fishes?"

"I will lie in the cool of the water by day, and at night time I will browse along the banks of the rivers, and in the vleis," replied the hippopotamus. "I promise that I will not eat your little fishes."

"But that will not be proof to me that you are keeping your promise!" pointed out The Great Lord N'gai.

"Well then," answered the hippopotamus, "I will come out of the water every time that food passes through my body, and I will scatter my dung on the earth with my tail. All that I have eaten will be spread out in your sight, and you will see for yourself that there are no fish bones. Surely this will be proof enough!"

So this is way, to this very day, the hippopotamus comes out of the water to scatter its dung as it looks up to heaven and says, "Look N'gai, no fishes!"

Narrator: Gwido Mariko

THE WIZARD'S BRIDE

KIKUYU

In the days of long ago, when wizards practised magic and evil doings upon the earth, there lived a very handsome man. So dazzlingly handsome was he, in fact, that every maiden who set eyes upon him, fell hopelessly in love. True, word went around the countryside of lovely girls who mysteriously disappeared; but as there was talk of ugly cannibals and ogres who roamed the country, no one suspected this kind young man of kidnapping them.

Our tale begins upon a sunny spring morning when Wiweru, the lovely daughter of a Kikuyu chief, washed her cooking pots in the river that flowed not far from her father's home and, as she looked up, saw a handsome stranger watching her. "Lovely One," he sighed, with a smile and a flash of flawless teeth that captured her heart, "your hands are too beautiful to be spoilt with the work of a common slave. With such dignity and loveliness you should have those who wait upon you."

Wiweru was a strong-willed girl, who had so far refused to marry anyone of the many men her father had chosen for her. The old chief was so fond of his beautiful daughter that he let her have her own way. But Wiweru had never set eyes upon anyone so handsome or so captivating as the young man who now gazed at her across the water. She immediately fell deeply in love with him.

However, the girl was clever as well as beautiful, so rather than show her feelings to the stranger at this early stage, she replied haughtily, "Bold stranger, you speak to the daughter of this country's noble chief! Many have sought my hand, and none has won me. I would advise you to go and sow your compliments upon more fertile ground," and, taking up her pots, she turned her back upon the man and hastened home.

As time went on, Wiweru thought more and more about the bold, good-looking stranger and, for many days she lingered at the riverside, hoping that he would pass that way again.

The wizard, (for so he was), could afford to wait as he knew that he had already bewitched her by his magic arts. He continued to watch her secretly from his hiding-place among the reeds and rushes across the pool, and each time he saw her, his power over her increased. "Even without the spell that I have cast upon her, she could not resist my charms!" he chuckled to himself, until at last he revealed himself.

"The days have been empty since I last saw you, Lovely One," he murmured. "Tell me, what makes you again come unattended to this lonely place? You should have a husband who would see that you are guarded from the dangers that threaten lovely maidens such as you. I wish I could take this pleasant duty upon myself," he sighed.

This time Wiweru was kinder to the handsome stranger, and they began to meet each day at the water's edge until he agreed to ask her father's permission to marry her. "No, my daughter," said the old chief when they had talked, "I will not give my consent to such a marriage, for in my heart I know that this man's handsome face is a mask which hides a wicked heart."

Wiweru was angry and frustrated at her father's stern refusal, but as she was under the magician's spell, she was unable to resist him. She continued to meet her lover by the riverside until, finally, she agreed to run away with him. Far, far through the forest and over the plains, he took her – away to the North and there, at his home, made her his queen.

"Who could be more gentle and considerate than my lord?" she asked herself, after several weeks of married life. "I have only to wish for something and it is here. Life is indeed all that he promised me." She had many slaves to wait upon her, and life was pleasant. There was plenty of her favourite food, and each day her lover stroked her arms as he watched her satiny skin take on a richer bloom.

"My beloved Queen," he said to her one day, playfully pinching her plump arm, "our happiness must be celebrated by a feast for all my friends. There are many whom I would like you to meet. Tomorrow I will go hunting in the forest for meat for our banquet. You must remain at home and attend to the brewing of the beer. Be sure that your maidens prepare our largest cooking pot, and tell them to gather plenty of firewood ready for my return. This must be an occasion that all my friends remember!"

Off went the wicked wizard and visited all his cannibal friends, inviting them all to a mighty feast of human flesh – the main course of which, he told them, would be provided by his lovely bride. "I can promise you," he assured them one by one, "that she will be the most tender and toothsome morsel that you have ever tasted!"

It was lucky for Wiweru that a humble herd-boy was guarding his father's cattle in a field near where one of the guests lived. As the boy rested beneath the shade of a tree, he heard two men excitedly discussing their invitation. "Yes," said one of them, "the husband tells me that she has been fattened since she ran away with him, and he has left her at home to prepare the very pot in which she will be cooked. What an amusing situation!" and the two laughed cruelly at the wizard's trickery.

"This must be some evil plan," said the tender-hearted herd-boy to himself "I shall go and warn her!" and, calling a younger brother to care for his father's beasts, the herd-boy hastened to the wizard's home.

Here, he found everyone busy. Wiweru had seen to the brewing of a large supply of luscious beer, and there was wood piled high ready to cook the meat when it arrived. She was most excited as the party drew nearer. All was ready, except the main course – and that, her husband had assured her, he would bring from the forest with him, and he had never failed her yet. "He will have to hurry," she said to her servants, "for I can see some of the guests in sight." She pointed to some figures in the distance.

"Now," said the herd-boy to himself, "it's time I told her of the conversation I heard!" and he hurried forward to whisper in her ear.

At first Wiweru refused to believe the tale he told her but, after watching the sly way her many woman servants were glancing at her, the girl became suspicious. Then, as she saw her own over-plump arms and bulging body, the whole of her wicked husband's plot became clear to her.

"Surely the good Lord will have pity upon me!" cried the terrified bride, wringing her hands in dismay. And, sure enough, her cries for help were heard by The Great One for, at that very moment, a magic sleigh, drawn by two snow-white oxen, came gliding over the treetops, to stop at their feet.

The woman attendants screamed with rage as they rushed forward to catch Wiweru. Fortunately, their pursuers were too late, for the girl and boy flung themselves on to the magic sleigh in time to escape the angry women's hands. As the sleigh flew high over the treetops, the two of them looked down to see far, far beneath them, the wizard leading a party of guests to his home.

Very quickly, quarrels and arguments broke out. "My friend," grumbled the most important guest as he gazed into the empty cooking pot, "you invited us to a feast of human flesh, and all we find is an empty pot. Where is the feast?"

"Listen to me!" the unhappy wizard cried, "I do assure you that I am speaking the truth. Some magic has taken her away!"

"It's no concern of ours whether or not you speak the truth," argued his guests angrily. "We came, at your invitation, to eat human flesh, and we will not leave until we have had it!" Immediately they seized the protesting wizard and threw him into the big cooking pot where it boiled upon the fire and, although he proved to be a great deal tougher than his lovely bride would have been, his cannibal friends enjoyed their feast.

Meanwhile, the magic sleigh carried Wiweru and the herd-boy away over the treetops. There was great rejoicing and excitement as the girl and boy came down through the air right at the door of the old chief's hut, and he saw his beloved long-lost daughter jump from the magic sleigh and run to greet him. So delighted was he at her safe return that, after hearing of her narrow escape, the old man readily forgave Wiweru for her disobedience, for he had thought she was dead.

The brave, quick-thinking herd-boy was widely praised and, as a reward for defeating the wicked wizard's plan he was put in charge of the old chief's vast herd of cattle. Eventually he grew in importance to such an extent that he became the chief's Head Councillor, and married into the Royal Household. But he never did marry Wiweru.

Narrator: Gwido Mariko

KIMWAKI AND THE WEAVER BIRDS

KIKUYU

As an old Kikuyu man lay dying, he sent for his only son Kimwaki. "My son," he said, "I have lived my life, and the time has come for me to join my ancestors. In all these years I have not been idle. My fields are the fairest in the land, my cows are fat and healthy, and my goats are many. All these now belong to you. Carry me out and let me lie under the stars, for it is time for me to die."

So he died, and when the burial ceremonies had taken place, Kimwaki looked around him, and counted his wealth. He found that he was even richer than he had hoped, and he was young enough to enjoy it. No need for him to work anymore – and no one to nag him either. Life was very good, and he settled down to enjoy it as lazily as he could.

Day after day he lay dreaming in the sunshine or, when the sun became too hot for comfort, in the shade of a big tree that grew beside his hut. His fine fields became overgrown with weeds and grass. His sleek and glossy cattle became hollow-eyed and thin for no one drove them to the pastures. The little goats bleated in distress, not knowing where to go.

But Kimwaki did not care, for, with the great stores of food that had been provided by his father's work and wisdom, he felt he could well afford to sit back and rest. No fear of hunger could touch him.

In a land where it is the rule for each neighbour to help the other, this idle young man helped nobody, so nobody lifted one finger to help him. In this way, all that he had inherited went from bad to worse; no one cared, and he was avoided by all around him.

For many months Kimwaki led this useless life, until the loneliness bored him. Then, one day in the early spring, as he lay drowsing as usual under his tree, he heard excited twitterings from above. He opened his eyes in annoyance, to see what had disturbed his pleasant sleep and there, up in the tree, was a flock of little weaver birds. They were darting hither and thither, as busy as could be, for it was nesting time.

Spring was in the air, and the males were building homes for their young families when they hatched. Their excited chattering caused him to open his eyes a little wider. He watched as they worked together, until he understood their joy.

Singing and laughing, each bird made his contribution to the weaver colony. One would bring a tiny piece of grass, another a little twig, while yet another added a feather to his nest.

They worked as though their very lives depended upon their haste and, when evening came, the frames of the little nests were finished.

On the following day the work continued: the birds' clever, tiny beaks wove the grasses in and out, lining the nests with softest down. Kimwaki watched it all, as he lay beneath the big tree. Thunder clouds were gathering in the sky, and when the second evening came, Kimwaki thought how wise the little birds were to provide shelter for their babies from the coming rain.

Every day now, he watched the feathered workers, until in a short while a whole colony of finished nests hung from the branches of his tree. And, during all this time, the lesson of their co-operation and their hard work had been sinking deeper and deeper into his mind.

Finally Kimwaki said to himself, as he listened to their cheerful chatter, "I am a strong young man, while they are only tiny birds. I have two big hands with which to work, while each of them has only a little beak. They are safe and sheltered, which I am not. They are the wise ones, and I am not!"

He thought the matter over during the night, and next morning he rose early, took his rusty hoe with him, and went to the field belonging to his nearest neighbour. There he began to dig and clear the weeds and grass away and, when this was done, he hoed the ground. All day long he worked beside the others had who joined him and, when evening came, he found himself singing as he retraced his steps to his broken-down hut. He felt as happy and light-hearted as the little weaver birds!

Day after day he went, first to the field of one neighbour, and then to another, helping where he could, and asking nothing in return. Then one morning, he awoke to hear cheerful chattering and laughter upon his own untidy, overgrown fields. He looked out and saw that his neighbours were as busy as could be, clearing and hoeing his weed-covered lands. He joined them at once, and soon the plot was ready for planting. And, later on, when the rains came, the same neighbours helped him to plant his crops and to re-thatch his leaking hut.

The months went by, and as the crops grew – mealies, beans and potatoes, so grew also his own pride. He no longer lazed away the days under the big tree, but continued to help those around him, and looked after his neglected flocks. Joyfully he watched the glow of health creep back to the dull coats of his cows and goats.

Before long his crops were ready to be harvested, and willing hands helped him to reap them – returning the help that Kimwaki had so willingly given to them. And when all the grain had been stored away, and his potatoes and beans sold, he found, to his joy, that once more his father's fields were the richest in the land.

Kimwaki looked up and gave thanks to the little weaver birds, for showing him that only through unselfishness and hard work can peace and happiness be found.

THE BUSHBUCK'S HOUSE

KIKUYU

Once upon a time a bushbuck lived in a neat little house on the bank of a river. After paying a visit to his friend the goat one day, the bushbuck returned to his home to find his front door shut. A strange and very harsh voice was coming from inside. "Who is inside my house?" asked the bushbuck.

"It is I, the eater of bushbucks," replied a rasping voice. "Beware, for I am coming out to eat you!"

The bushbuck was greatly alarmed and he ran as fast as his legs would carry him to tell his friend the goat about the dreadful monster in his house. On his way he met an elephant. "Friend," exclaimed the elephant in surprise, "I have never seen anyone so frightened as you. Why are you in such a hurry on this fine and sunny morning?"

"There is a wicked monster in my house," panted the bushbuck, "who says that he is coming out to eat me!"

The elephant laughed loudly at the bushbuck's fear. "What utter nonsense," he said. "I will go and see for myself." So the elephant went boldly towards the river, while the bushbuck kept well away. "Who is inside the bushbuck's house?" the elephant called out from a distance.

He was greeted by a throaty voice which croaked, "It is I, the eater of elephants. Beware, for I am coming out to eat you!" The elephant thought, by the sound of the voice, that this must be an even larger monster than himself so he tore off into the forest with his trunk in the air, knocking down trees left and right in his haste, while the bushbuck pelted along ahead of him.

They had not gone far before they met a lion. "Well, well, well! my friend," said the lion in surprise. "Whoever has had the impertinence to frighten such a big creature as you?"

"There is a terrible monster in the bushbuck's house," stammered the elephant. "I – I laughed at the bushbuck when he told me this, good Lion, but now I know that he spoke the truth, and he was quite right to be afraid. A dreadful monster, good friend Lion!"

"Come," said the lion good-naturedly, "the three of us will go together to see who dares to threaten the creatures of the forest."

After a great deal of persuasion the two trembling animals agreed to return with the lion to investigate the matter. All three made their way to the little house by the river. "Who is in the bushbuck's house?" roared the lion in a thunderous voice.

"It is I, the eater of lions!" came the harsh, grating reply. "Beware, for I am coming out to eat you!"

"WHAT! TO EAT THE KING OF THE FOREST?" bellowed the lion. "Then come out and eat me, for I am not afraid of you!"

There was muffled laughter from inside the hut, and the lion pushed aside the door to see a fat old frog sitting in the middle of the floor, chuckling and croaking to himself. "So," said the lion, greatly amused, "you are the 'dangerous monster' who has dared to frighten my two friends?" It wasn't long before all the animals of the forest heard how cowardly the bushbuck and the elephant had been, and needless to say they laughed at their own cowardice!

From that day onward, the elephant has been ashamed of himself, and admits that the lion is king of the animals, even though the elephant is the largest creature in the wilds.

THE CHAMELEON'S
FALL FROM
GRACE

KIKUYU

This unfortunate happening took place a long, long while ago: so long ago, in fact, that there was only one Man on the Earth, and he lived under the towering crags of lovely Mount Kenya. There were several women to wait upon him, but they didn't count – and, in any case, that was a state of affairs that Man looked upon as his right.

It is true that the Great God N'gai had placed many other living creatures on the Earth; four-legged animals, birds, reptiles and insects, as well as the cold-blooded fish in the rivers, lakes and streams. But of the human male, the most important and perfect of all the labour of his hands, there was only Man himself.

Throughout the hours of daylight the Sun, N'gai's most trusted servant, watched over all his children. Without fail, the Sun rose regularly above the tree-tops at the same hour each morning, shedding light and warmth upon the Earth. He must surely be male, for all his actions could be relied upon.

But not so the Moon. "She can only be a woman," thought the Man, as he gazed at the sky, "for she never arrives or departs at the same time for two days running!" He would watch her silvery radiance grow smaller and smaller until she disappeared altogether sometimes, and these nights were dark indeed. "Most unsatisfactory," thought the Man, so he sent a message to N'gai about it.

The Man had another complaint too. As time passed, and more humans were born on the Earth, Man found that death came to claim many of those who were both dear and useful to him. He came to realise that human life was limited. The fact that animals died was an entirely different matter, for had not the good N'gai put animals on earth for the benefit of Man? For these creatures, death had to come. How else could Man eat? But surely the Great God N'gai should allow Man the gift of immortality!

N'gai listened to these complaints with interest, and for a long while he thought deeply upon the two matters. Eventually he called the chameleon to him. "Go, my child," N'gai instructed the little creature, "and take this message to 'the two-legged-one' who lives beneath the topmost crags of our Mother Mountain."

The chameleon was an obliging little reptile and, with the message rolled in a leaf and clasped by the end of his long curly tail, left cheerfully to obey his Creator's command.

The sun was shining brightly, and the lazy feeling of spring was in the air. Sweet-scented flowers and singing birds were all around him, as he hurried upon his way. The scent of flowers, of course, attracted insects – and insects for the chameleon meant food.

The chameleon remembered that it was a long while since he had eaten, and eventually he spotted a particularly plump and toothsome mantis. Such a meal would fill a chameleon's stomach for a long time. So our little messenger left the path that he was following, and as the mantis followed a butterfly, so the chameleon followed the mantis. He was soon caught up in such an exciting chase that he forget all about the task he had been given.

The butterfly flitted from flower to flower, and the mantis chased it, just out of reach of the chameleon's long, sticky tongue. Suddenly, before he realised how he had got there, N'gai's trusted messenger found himself racing down a dark and twisting ant-bear hole.

Deeper and deeper into the earth he went until, finally, he found himself among a host of ugly, frightening creatures. It did not take him long to realise that he had reached the dreaded Underworld.

The chameleon had many desperate adventures before he escaped from this fearful place, including some narrow escapes from cannibal giants of his own kind – and it was a long, long while before he remembered the rolled-up leaf that he still grasped so tightly in the curl at the end of his elegant tail.

At the thought of the punishment that Great N'gai would give him for his disobedience, the little chameleon felt a prickly, tingling sensation steal all over his body. His skin turned from its normal bright green colour to a sickly yellow. Who knows? This might have been how the chameleon became able to change his colour in order to hide from those he fears.

It took N'gai's messenger many weeks to find his way back to the sunlight and safety of the Upper World, where he was met by a very angry Lord of All Things.

"What have you been doing this long while?" asked N'gai, in a voice of thunder. "From now onwards and for ever more, you will be looked down upon and cursed by man, because the message that you carried to him was the gift of immortality. My message would also have saved the Moon from her time of banishment from the heavens each month. Now it is too late. Because of your disobedience, Man shall continue to die, and the Moon shall for ever leave the sky from month to month. Go, you are disgraced for ever more!"

And that is the reason why the chameleon is hated not only in Kikuyuland, but in many other parts of Africa as well.

HOW THE OSTRICH GOT HIS LONG NECK

KIKUYU

Mr. Ostrich was a sober-minded, serious husband, who was always willing to assist his wife in her family duties. "My dear," he said to her one evening, when their large clutch of eggs seemed almost ready to hatch, "my black feathers cannot be seen in the darkness, so I will guard our eggs by night, and at the same time keep them warm for you. That will leave you free to relax and enjoy yourself until daybreak each morning."

He settled down clumsily to his unaccustomed task, while his flighty wife was more than thankful to be relieved of a duty which she already found a trial. She fluffed up her feathers and, to show how pleased she was, she set off in a joyful high-stepping dance among the low termite-mounds that surrounded their nest.

The big birds had chosen the site with care, for they knew that a sitting ostrich hen, with her head down, looks from the distance like a grey mound of earth. They had decided to rear their young on the short-grassed plain lands because they could see all round them, for in those days the ostrich had a short neck like a guinea-fowl and partridge. They had learned the hard lesson that in long grass their enemies could attack them before they realised their danger.

To keep their precious eggs safe from the dreaded fires that swept across the plains, the two birds had carefully scratched away a broad band of dusty earth in the grass round the slight hollow that was their nest. On the whole they were a happy pair, although from time to time the husband had disapproved of his wife's high-spirited ways. At this particular time, she should behave more sensibly as she had her eggs to look after. He wriggled his massive thighs on the ground as he had seen his wife do, to shift the position of the eggs so that they lay more comfortably in their bed, and settled down to his long night's wait.

It was full moon. The silvery light shed strange shadows and threw up ghostly figures among the surrounding mounds of earth. His head was beginning to nod with weariness, when he became aware of his wife's hissing laugh. He was wide awake in a moment. Straining his short neck to its utmost limit, he saw her dodging in and out between the termite-mounds in a wild game of hide-and-seek with a handsome young ostrich in hot pursuit.

This would never do. He half rose from the nest – but sank down again with a sigh. He dare not leave the precious eggs, whatever the reason. What if they were to grow cold while he went to tell his flirting wife what he thought of her disgraceful behaviour?

He settled down again with a feeling of annoyance, but strained his neck further and further, to try to catch sight of her as she dodged and raced between the termite-mounds on the moonlit veld.

From time to time he did catch a glimpse of her, and heard her foolish giggles – and each time that he did so, he strained and stretched his neck trying to see further and yet further between the nearby termite-mounds. At last, the long, tedious night came to an end. As it did so, his wife appeared out of the grey distance to take over her duties once more.

The ostrich rose stiffly, prepared to punish his wife for her undignified behaviour; but as he did so, he felt a strangeness in the muscles of his neck. He looked down at his feet, and was alarmed to discover how very far away from his head they were – and he realised with a shock that, as a result of all the straining that he had done during the long night, his neck had stretched, and stretched, and stretched. He tried to shake it back to its former length, but no matter what he did, it stayed just the same: he had stretched beyond return.

And that is why the ostrich has a long neck – a lasting memory of a flighty wife.

THE HYENA AND THE CALF

KIKUYU

On the slopes of Mount Kenya, the animals once called a meeting to discuss the lack of gratitude among many of the creatures of the wilds.

"We should give thanks, to the Great Lord N'gai, for all the good food that he puts before us," said King Lion, "for how can we expect him to provide us with food every day, if we do not show our gratitude? Surely those who fail to praise his goodness will have these gifts taken from them one day!"

The animals nodded their heads in agreement, for the Good Lord N'gai was indeed the Father of them all and, as food had been scarce for some time, they had begun to wonder if they had not taken his favours too much for granted? The meeting ended, and the animals returned to their homes, determined to improve their manners in the future.

Not long after this, the greedy hyena was walking along a path, when he came upon a calf tied to a tree by a strip of hide. "This must be a present from Good Lord N'gai," he said to himself "Who else could have put this calf here for me to eat?" and he smacked his lips at the thought of the splendid meal ahead of him.

In his excitement, however, he forgot to give thanks to N'gai for leading him to such a rich feast. "Where," he wondered, "shall I begin my meal. Shall I start with this tender calf and leave the hard dry hide round its neck to the end? Or should I leave the calf to the last?"

He thought over the problem and decided to eat the hide first, thinking that he could enjoy looking forward to the pleasure of the tender second course even longer. "Yes," he said to himself, "this is a real feast. I will eat the hard, dry hide first, and then I will eat the calf."

He set to work with his powerful jaws, close to the poor calf's neck, and as he swallowed the lumps of indigestible rawhide, he got nearer and nearer to the tree to which the calf had been tied. The foolish creature was so occupied with thoughts of his meal, that he did not notice that the calf, no longer tied up, had lost no time in returning to its owner's hut.

Only then did the greedy creature remember that Lord N'gai had given him a generous meal, and he had failed to say thank-you. He hastily did so, and called loudly to N'gai to make the calf stand still, so that he could catch up with it. But as so often happens in life, the hyena was not given a second chance. The calf reached the safety of its owner's hut, while the ungrateful hyena had to be content with the piece of hard hide for his supper.

Now, every time you hear the hyena's mournful cry in the stillness of the night, you will know that the greedy animal is asking the Good Lord N'gai to give him back the calf that he was stupid enough to lose.

WANJOHI AND THE BIRD

MALAWI

Long, long ago, there lived a poor man called Wanjohi and his wife. They were so poor that he had to go searching in the forests for food to eat. Sometimes it would mean only a meal of roots and berries, but occasionally Wanjohi was lucky enough to catch a bird or animal in one of the traps and snares he set.

There was, however, a large and very beautiful bird which had proved too clever to be tempted into even his most carefully hidden traps. Besides this, it seemed to mock him as he saw it every day, cleverly just out of range of his bow and arrow. Eventually he determined to capture it.

One day, when Wanjohi was on the point of returning home empty-handed and even more hungry than usual, he remembered a trap that he had failed to visit. He retraced his steps and gave a shout of joy for there, securely caught by a leg, was the lovely creature that had escaped him so often.

He rushed forward and seized the bird by the neck. "Today I have got you, my friend!" he cried and took out his knife to kill it. He would have at least something, if only a bird, to take back to his wife that evening.

"Mercy, human, mercy!" spluttered the poor creature, as the grip upon its throat tightened. "Spare my life, and I promise that you will not regret your kindness."

The man loosened his grasp and stepped back in surprise. This rare, golden plumaged creature could actually talk! "Although my only earthly possessions are these golden feathers, yet in them lies a magic that will provide you with both food and drink for ever more. Set me free, good human, for this noose has cut painfully into my leg."

Now here was a problem indeed. What if the bird was lying? He would lose the precious food that would keep himself and his wife from hunger: and yet, the bird itself might also have a wife – and maybe even babies – waiting for his return as anxiously as his own dear wife.

Suppose the bird spoke the truth? Why, he would be able to sit back in idleness for ever. Surely he could trust a bird that spoke like a man? Wanjohi decided to risk it, and untied the snare that had bitten so deeply into the poor creature's leg.

Thankfully the lovely bird stretched its aching limbs then, carefully pulling a golden-coloured feather from each wing, it gave them to him. "With this gift, human," it said, "I also give you words of warning: if you wish to keep the magic of these feathers, you must never speak to others of your good fortune. Should you do so, their power will vanish, and you will be left as poor as you are today. Do not treat my warning lightly. Hold these feathers in your hands and wish, and they will give you your heart's desires."

The man thanked the bird for its gift and hastened home, wishing as he hurried along the path that he would find plenty of food waiting for him at his journey's end. Which would he find, he wondered – starvation, or riches?

The golden bird was as good as its word, for inside Wanjohi's hut the pots and bowls were full to overflowing, while the dried-up spring nearby gushed out with sparkling waters once more, so that his wife no longer had to walk miles to the only water-hole they knew. Life smiled upon the couple at last, and Wanjohi was able to relax for the first time in his life, just making a wish for all the things that made life sweet – and they arrived out of mid-air.

Many times the woman questioned her husband how it happened that their mealie patch was not ploughed or weeded and he no longer hunted in the forest, yet she always found plenty of food in her cooking pots? But each time she asked him, he refused to explain.

At last, as so often happens when life becomes too easy, Wanjohi grew careless of what he said, boasting to all about his wealth, so that the woman grew increasingly suspicious. "Husband," she said in exasperation, "you never seem surprised at our wealth. You must be hiding something from me. Maybe at night-time while I sleep, you steal the good things that I find cooking upon the fire. I think you are friends with the Evil One, for who else can bring sparkling water bubbling from the parched earth, when all else is dry? I shall ask the witch-doctor to smell out this evil."

Now, the very mention of a witch-doctor smelling out evil struck terror into the heart of her simple husband, who had no wish for things he did not understand. "Wife," begged Wanjohi, "do not do so. For he is sure to discover the magic feathers that provide us with all these good things. You could even lose your husband who has brought you such a comfortable life, for the witch-doctor might kill me to obtain the magic of my golden feathers for himself."

Too late he remembered the bird's warning. Not only had he now shared his secret with his wife, but he had also boasted to others of his riches. Wanjohi had little hope when he held the feathers and wished his daily wishes next day, and his worst fears came true as he found that nothing happened. Even the bubbling spring was now only drying mud.

Once more the couple knew what it was to go hungry, and Wanjohi went back to setting traps along the game-paths in the forest as he used to do. Life was even harder than before, for drought now made food still more difficult to find. However, one day while visiting his traps as usual, he met a neighbour with his dog. "Let us hunt together," said Wanjohi, pleased to have company. To his great surprise they found the same golden bird, caught in one of his particularly well-hidden snares.

Wanjohi rushed towards it exclaiming, "Once more you are in my power golden bird! I have caught you once again! Give me two more of your magic feathers, and I will let you go."

"Spare me this second time, good human!" begged the bird, as he at once untied the noose that held it. But no sooner had he set the poor creature free, than his neighbour's dog pounced on it. Dragging the animal away with difficulty, Wanjohi hastily picked up the bird and ran to the edge of the forest to release it, without waiting for any gift of feathers.

"Once more, human, I thank you," said the bird gratefully. "If you had not helped, the dog would have killed me. When we first met I made you a gift of my magic feathers because you spared my life although you and your wife were hungry. You broke the condition I made, but that is no concern of mine. You suffered for not listening to my warning, and maybe you have learned your lesson.

"This time I will give you all that is in my power to give, and I make no condition with my gift. The magic in these feathers will last for ever, for you have not only spared my life – you have saved it." Plucking two more feathers, one from each wing, the bird gave them to Wanjohi. Then, spreading its golden wings, it rose up into the heavens and was gone.

It was a very happy man who returned to his wife that day – happy at his repeated good fortune, grateful to the golden bird, and wiser for knowing that kindness to one in trouble can bring its own reward.

"COOK, EAT AND CARRY ME"

KIKUYU

A man once lived with his wife and two young daughters. The elder daughter was good, kind and beautiful, and everyone loved her. The younger daughter, however, was just the opposite, besides which, she was always jealous of her elder sister.

One afternoon the mother sent Gethui, the elder daughter, to fetch water from the river. Down the path sped Gethui, with the big water gourd slung upon her back. She sang happily as she went, for there was laughter in the air, and life was good.

She reached the river and, bending over the water, dipped the gourd into its sparkling clearness. She was about to draw it up again, when some unseen power pulled it downwards. Now, although Gethui was frightened of the underwater world, she was even more frightened of her father's anger, for he was a cruel man. And, as she dared not return without his precious gourd, she held onto it with all her strength.

Slowly, but relentlessly, she was dragged down to the bottom of the crystal-clear pool. There, the same unseen force pulled both the gourd and herself into a large cave in the side of the bank. To her great surprise Gethui saw a pot of food cooking merrily in the shadows, and heard a strange-sounding voice from inside it saying, "Cook, eat and carry me!"

The food looked so tempting, and smelt so good, that Gethui remembered it was a long while since she had eaten. So, without waiting for a second invitation, she sat down and began to eat. "What tasty mealies!" she thought, and then looked around, hoping to thank the owner of the food. Seeing no one, she lifted the pot to her shoulder and was about to go back to the pool, when a voice from another pot, which was also cooking merrily by itself, called out, "Cook, eat and carry me!"

The smell that wafted to her nostrils was even more tempting than that of the first pot, so she lost no time in sitting down to taste this one as well. "I must not insult the one who offers me such fine food by refusing to eat it," she said to herself "Truly, these are the most delicious yams that I have ever tasted. A thousand blessings upon the giver!"

When she had eaten well from the second pot, she was about to lift it, too, onto her shoulder, when she saw an old man beckoning to her – and beside him were two clay pots. Gethui approached him hastily, prepared to thank him for the delicious meal that surely he must have provided, when he spoke to her. "My child," he said, "I have yet another gift for you to take back to the upper world with you, for I see by your modesty and good manners that you deserve it. Take your choice of these two pots, and my blessing upon your choice."

Gethui was so overcome by all the good fortune that had already come her way, and she did not wish to appear greedy. She chose the small, uninteresting-looking pot and, thanking the old man, she returned through the water to the dry land above.

Then she gazed with wonder at the contents of the clay pot she had chosen, and her eyes opened wide in astonishment as she drew from it an unending supply of beaded ornaments, bangles, clothes, and all the lovely things that she had only dreamed of in the past. She felt rich beyond her wildest dreams!

But what would her father say, she wondered, when he saw all her new possessions? Would he believe her when she told him where they had come from? He would probably say that she had stolen them. They had better be hidden.

She waited until darkness came and then she upset her water pot on the fire in the hut, so that it was all dark inside. "What's made you so clumsy?" her mother scolded; hurrying out of the hut to find some dry wood.

Then, while her mother was busy relighting the fire, Gethui smuggled in her hoard of treasures and hid them in the thatch among the rafters, while she assured her parents that the pots of food were a gift from the "Old Man of the River", and they finally allowed her to keep them.

However, Gethui's pretty treasures were eventually found, and when, in spite of many punishments she still insisted that the Old Man of the River had given them to her, they believed her.

This was enough to make the younger daughter decide that she, too, would visit the underwater world. "I will claim hospitality from the Old Man of the River," she said to herself, "and beg for pretty ornaments. Why should my elder sister have all the good things in life, as well as being so pretty?" So she took the water gourd as Gethui had done and went to the same pool on the following morning.

She threw the gourd into the water and, without waiting to see what happened, scrambled in after it. Looking around for the cave that Gethui had described, she saw the pot bubbling and cooking by itself. "Ah!" smiled the younger sister, "now I shall have my fill." Not waiting for an invitation, she sat down and ate until she had finished all the food inside it.

Rising from her feast, the greedy child saw the second pot, also cooking merrily. "This, too, must be meant for me!" she chuckled to herself, as she sat down beside it and began her second meal. Then, when her stomach was full, she looked around for the old man.

"There he is – the one who gave Gethui all her lovely gifts," she thought, as she saw him sitting by two clay pots in the distance. "Old man!" she shouted, rushing towards him, "what gifts have you got for me?"

"My child," replied the old man as the girl reached his side, "you have no modesty and no manners, but in spite of this, I will still offer you the choice of two gifts. Take the one that pleases you most, though you might be well advised to choose the smaller and my blessing with it."

However, the greedy girl was not in the mood for advice. "I will take the big one," she said rudely, "for it must hold more gifts and better ones than the smaller one." So, without a word of gratitude to the old man, the girl grabbed the larger of the two clay pots and, with her two empty food pots clutched to her as well, was soon back on the river bank. Here she lost no time in thrusting her hand inside the pot to see what she had been given.

But the pot that had looked the best from the outside, was the worst one inside, for it contained the germs of a swelling disease. Bigger she had wanted, so bigger she became. The infection at once attacked the girl's right hand and spread quickly up her arm. Soon it had reached her body, which swelled to an enormous size.

With screams of fear she ran to her parents' home, but when they saw her coming they cried out, "There's something dreadful coming! A monster! Run away, the land is cursed!" Without recognising their younger daughter, or waiting to gather up their belongings, the father, mother and Gethui fled in terror, leaving the greedy one alone with her troubles. And, as no one went back to find out, she may be there still.

KING LION AND KING EAGLE

XHOSA

One day a very long time ago, a young baboon was sitting under a tall spreading tree, scratching himself and thinking of nothing in particular.

Presently he became aware of voices drifting down from the topmost branches. He was a meddlesome creature, always ready to pry into other people's business, so he pricked up his ears and craned his neck until he caught sight of the speakers. Their conversation interested him, for they were talking about his lord, the King of Beasts.

He peered upwards and could just see a gaunt, bare-necked vulture talking to King Eagle. "Lord of all Feathered Things," said the vulture, bending his scraggy neck in respect, "no one on earth or in the sky can compare with you. Why do you allow another to say he is a king? Oh, your Feathered Mightiness, no one should dare to challenge your right to rule all things that breathe. Yet that upstart of a lion down below roars boldly that he is king of all!"

King Eagle nodded his head in agreement. "My good Chief Councillor, no one is better fitted to rule than I for, from the heights of the sky, I can safeguard my people from any danger that threatens them. My might is in the strength of my tireless wings. Who can soar to greater heights than I, or see as far?"

"True, oh King," replied the vulture, "whereas the foolish lion, from his humble position on the ground, can scarcely see beyond his nose. Many is the time his four-footed subjects have been killed by hunters, and never a word of warning has he been able to give them. Trouble is upon them before he is aware of it. With you, my lord, every danger is seen from where you hover in the sky, and your feathered subjects are duly warned." The eagle preened his feathers and then asked, "Is he, in your opinion, as handsome as I am?"

"Not in all the heavens, your Magnificence!" answered the vulture, wriggling his neck in his desire to please. "He is a drab-looking creature with all that long hair around his neck. While you, oh King!, your wings shine like a royal gown with golden medals, your noble head is crowned with feathers, and the shining black upon your well-groomed body glistens like the blades of spears!"

The eagle's eyes shone with excitement at his councillor's praise. "How right you are!" he broke in. "Why should I stand this lion's cheek? I will declare war upon the fellow, and make him bow before me!"

This was too much for the baboon, who burst out laughing and shouted up, "What fools you are to think that a bird could ever rule over one as mighty as our lord, King Lion. Your councillor's little head could never contain such wisdom as that of his chief councillor, the elephant. Do you usually crack jokes like this so early in the morning?"

The baboon was well known for his bad manners, but this was too much for the two birds. They flew away in disgust, back to the eagle's home in the mountain crags, where the King of Birds at once sent word to his subjects to attend a meeting. Birds, insects – all flying things – came in flocks to hear his words, for he was a good ruler, and they were proud and willing to obey his commands.

"My people," he began, "both great and small" (at the last word he nodded his head graciously towards the insects), "I want each and every one of you to join me in a war to end the foolish boastings of the lion. He tells all creatures that he alone is king. As master of both air and earth, am not I more fitted to be the king of all living things?"

"Hear, hear! You are, you are!" they cried with one voice and clamoured for the honour of fighting for their king – all, that is, except the bat. He had never been very keen on fighting; but since the bat is more animal than bird, the eagle decided to do without him.

In the meantime the baboon had found the lion and said to him, "Your Majesty, King of Beasts, listen I pray to your humble subject." The lion inclined his head, surprised how polite the baboon could be when he wanted to. "While minding my own business as usual in the forest just now, I heard the eagle talking to that scavenging councillor of his, the vulture. He was boasting that he is the noblest king on earth, and said that you, my lord, were nothing as compared to him. He was most rude too about your looks, and was busy making plans to make you bow down to him in homage."

"My hair and hide!" spluttered His Majesty in a fury. "We will be ready for him," and immediately sent messengers to call his people and tell them to prepare for war.

Just as King Lion finished his speech, the bat flew in, very out of breath. "I bring you important news, Your Majesty," he squeaked. "I have just come from a meeting of the winged creatures. They plan to attack you in great force tomorrow – so be prepared to defend your throne."

"I am grateful for the warning that you so kindly bring," said the lion, "but I have no further use for you. You have wings, and you might easily fly back to the other creatures of the air with news of our intentions. No, there is no place for you amongst my troops." Not wanted by either side, the bat hung himself upside down under a tree and burst into tears.

As the king surveyed his troops, the faint-hearted jackal felt uncomfortable as he realised that the lion's gaze had fallen upon him. "My friend," said the King of Beasts, "I know that you are clever but I also know that you are much too great a coward to fight. What part do you propose to take in the coming battle?"

"Your Majesty," replied the jackal, "give me the honour to be your Flag Bearer! And since we have no flag to fly, allow my tail to take the place of one. I will stand upon a rock that overlooks the battle, and will hold my tail high as long as we are winning. I will only lower my tail if you are losing."

"That is hardly likely, my good fellow," the lion replied distrustfully. "But none of your tricks, please!"

Early the following morning a tremendous whirring of wings was heard. It was King Eagle, attacking with his airborne troops. All the creatures of the air were there – even the insects were taking part.

But King Lion had not been slow in assembling his forces. All creatures of the earth had come to fight beneath his banner: frogs, snakes, lizards – everyone was present. The whirring of wings was soon drowned as the animals went to war. Snakes hissed as they struck upwards with their poison fangs to meet the birds that flew above. Lions roared, elephants trumpeted, wild-cats screamed – the noise was deafening as the battle raged backwards and forwards.

The winged army was gaining the upper hand, because many of those who fought on the ground had lost their eyes as their enemies swooped down from above. The insects, too, went for their eyes and blinded them. Over and over again the animals charged, determined not to give in. All the time they were encouraged by the rigid tail of their Flag Bearer.

Now the bat was still hanging upside down in his tree and sobbing. He really felt he deserved to be treated better after he had flown so far to warn the King of the Beasts. So when a bee buzzed up to him and asked what he was doing, he was glad of a friendly ear and told her everything that had happened – including the bit about the jackal's tail.

"Right!" hummed the bee. "Leave the rest to me. I'll teach them not to spurn a friend who warned them in their time of need!" She flew back to the eagle.

"Your Majesty," said the little bee to her feathered king, "I am going to put an end to this disgraceful fight, which has already lasted far too long. Allow me to show the animals that they are defeated."

"Excellent!" replied King Eagle. "I admire brave insects like you." So the bee flew straight to where the jackal stood on the highest point of a big rock and drove her sting securely into the softest part under the Flag Bearer's bushy tail.

Down came the flag at once! The jackal, screaming with agony, clapped his tail between his hind legs and tore off into the forest, with his ears lying flat on the back of his head. Seeing the flag fall with such speed, King Lion and all his subjects believed that the battle was truly lost. They turned and ran for their lives.

Sometime later peace was declared between the rival kings. The lion sent a humble request for his throne to be restored to him, politely suggesting that a bird was really too small to be king of all things.

But although the eagle agreed to give the lion back his throne he reminded him that since he had been completely and utterly defeated in war, he was never even to think that he was more powerful than His Majesty King Eagle, Ruler of All Flying Things – in spite of their difference in size.

Amid a great multitude of winged creatures, the eagle rose proudly into the air, while the lion and his earth-bound followers were left, ashamed and humbled on the plain below.

Narrator: Thandiwe Mceleni

THE FOUR FRIENDS

XHOSA

Ndlebende was a sad old donkey, with memories of those good times when he was well fed and well looked after. As his master's most useful servant, he had willingly carried heavy loads and allowed the children to climb on his back on their way to herding the cows. He even carried his master's heavy weight without complaint.

How different things were now, he thought, for he could not carry any load without stumbling. Life would not be too bad, even now, if only they would allow him to drowse away these last few years in peace. But the lush pastures were kept for those who worked. Only tasteless, frost-bitten grass for him.

Even worse, on that very morning he had heard his master grumble, "Wife, I can't stand that donkey's laziness any longer. Even beatings have no effect these days. He's useless, and just eats the grass that would feed our cows. Tomorrow I will have him killed."

There were tears in the old donkey's eyes when he overheard his master's plan. "I must leave this place at once," he decided, "before it is too late! I shall be safer among the wild creatures of the forest, than here." So after darkness had fallen, Ndlebende sadly stole away into the wild, wondering what the future had in store for him.

Caring little where he went, so long as it was away from human beings, he walked for several miles until, weary and worn, he lay down to rest. The sun rose clear and smiling on the following morning and he felt more cheerful. Off he went and soon he came upon a dog lying sadly under a bush. "At least here is a friendly face," he thought, so he asked, "Friend dog, why do you look so sorrowful on such a bright and pleasant morning?"

The dog sighed mournfully. "I have every reason to be sad," he whimpered. "This very morning I overheard my master tell his wife that as I am now too old to chase thieves when they prowl around his hut at night time, or to assist in the hunt, he intends to kill me. Do you wonder that I have left my home?"

"Well," said the donkey, "in that case, you and I have the same sort of trouble. Let's join together, and go travelling somewhere we will be safe from human beings." The dog gladly accepted the donkey's invitation, and the two continued upon their journey.

Before they had travelled far they heard a pitiful meowing close by. "Listen!" said the dog as they stopped. "Someone must be in worse trouble than either of us!" They hunted in the long grass and found a pathetically thin and mangy cat. "Hullo!" said the dog and donkey together, "what are you doing so far from human beings at this hour of the morning?"

"Hush!" gasped the cat, looking fearfully over his shoulder to make certain that he was not being followed, "I only just escaped alive. Last night while I was sleeping peacefully by the fire in my mistress's hut, I was woken by her telling her grandson to catch me and put me into a bag, and throw me into the river. She said that I am too old and feeble to earn my keep by catching rats – so why should I eat her food, and give nothing in return? Phew," he continued after a pause, "that was a narrow escape, for they nearly got me!" His sides still heaved from the running he had had to do.

"Then join us, friend cat," invited Ndlebende, "for the three of us are in the same plight. Come, we will seek peace in a new country." And the three old animals continued their journey together.

Their path led under a large, spreading tree, and there they saw a rooster sitting upon one of the overhanging branches. "What! you, too, so far from mankind! Tell us, friend rooster, why are you sitting up there?" asked the dog. The rooster gave a frightened look around him. "You did not see anyone with a knobkerrie in his hand, looking for me, did you?" he asked. "If I didn't have a little power left in these old wings, they would have knocked me over," he sighed with relief. "It was fortunate that I happened to overhear them deciding I should provide the family with their next meal. A great pot of water was steaming upon the fire, ready to put me into ... oh, it was dreadful!" and the poor bird shuddered at the memory of it.

A murmur of sympathy passed among the three travellers. "You are fortunate to have met us," said the donkey, "for we also have been forced to leave the safety of our masters' homes because we are too old. Join us, friend rooster, and the four of us will seek the happiness in old age that our masters would not allow."

The four animals, each happy with their new companionship, continued along the pathway in search of a place where they could end their lives in peace. But as the night closed down upon them, they realised that they had been travelling since the early dawn. They were tired, so they decided to rest until the morning.

Finding a suitable resting place beneath a tree, the donkey and the dog chose to sleep under its sheltering boughs, while the cat and the rooster preferred the safety of the higher branches. The rooster scrambled up until he reached the very top of the tree, where he prepared to settle for the night. "Well, well!" he exclaimed, after craning his neck to get a better view of the surroundings, "we are near to human habitation after all. We must be careful, for I see a light in the distance."

The cat and dog both heaved a sigh of relief because, of the four of them, only the donkey was accustomed to sleep without a shelter above his head, and the night was cold. The cat and dog therefore suggested that someone should be sent to the hut to investigate.

"The night air has already set me shivering," said the dog, "besides, we might find something to eat. It has been a long day without food."

The cat crept stealthily up to the hut and peeped inside. "Ssss-kat!" he spat when he returned to his friends. "It is a wicked place for they eat their own kind! There's no safety for us among people like this." And sure enough, they were cannibals. The floor was littered with human bones.

The rooster cleared his throat. "I have a plan," he said. "Let us drive these cannibals from their home, and then we can live there. You, Ndlebende, must stand on your hind legs with your front feet on the wall beside the door; you," and he turned to the dog, "must climb the donkey's back, with the cat on top of you, and I will perch on top of the cat's head. Then, we must all raise our voices as loudly as we can. We will soon have the owners of the hut running for their lives!"

The rooster was right. The cannibals took one terrified look at the strange, ghostly apparition which they thought was about to attack them and, without waiting to hear the end of the dreadful din that was coming from the four creatures, they rushed wildly into the night.

"Splendid!" the donkey congratulated the rooster. "Now, when they return, all four of us must attack them inside the hut. They will be far too frightened to return after a second shock." So, when each had eaten well from the food stored in the hut, the donkey settled down behind the door, while the dog stretched out beside him; the cat curled up in front of the fire, and the rooster perched on top of the half-closed door.

Some time passed before the dog heard the stealthy approach of the owners of the hut, and warned his companions to be ready for them. Quietly the leading cannibal crept in at the half-closed door and, seeing the cat's eyes glinting, he took them for the last spark of the fire.

He bent down to blow them back to life – but what a shock greeted him! The cat sprang into his face, scratching him with ten sharp claws, while the dog attacked his legs. He turned to escape only to be met by the donkey's hard hoofs and, as he reached the door, the rooster landed on his head and nearly pecked his eyes out. With yells of pain and terror the cannibals rushed from the hut and they all fled until they were far away from the fearful danger that lurked within their hut. The four friends lived in happiness and security in their own little home until they were separated by the ending that comes to us all, but not by the hand of man.

Narrator: Thandiwe Mceleni

Note: This story seems to be an adaptation from some early Mission school teaching. It is like an old German tale. However, it is apparently now looked upon by many Xhosa people as their own. The domestic cat did not come to the part of South Africa inhabited by the Xhosa people until early in the 19th Century, and the donkey even later.

# SANKATANE

LESOTHO

On the very top of the wild bare hills of Lesotho, there lived an enormous monster called Kholumolumo. One day he decided that he alone would occupy the land. So he left his hilltop home, and roamed the country far and wide, swallowing every man and beast he could find.

From hut to hut he went, and from kraal to kraal, eating everyone and everything. Nothing was left alive. At least that was what he intended, but their ancestors were watching over Masankatane, and her son Sankatane, as they slept beneath a mat in a lonely hut. Kholumolumo missed them in his search.

When they awoke, they went to gather food for the evening meal. A great stillness reigned over all the land. All the familiar sounds were gone. There were no songs or noises. No sounds of cattle lowing reached their ears, and they searched in vain for those they loved.

The days passed by, and still they found no sign of man nor beast, and their hearts were sad. One day Sankatane said, "Mother, where have all our people gone?"

Masankatane replied, "Only the monster Kholumolumo could have done this. He must have passed us over as we slept, otherwise we would have disappeared as well."

"Where does Kholumolumo live?" asked Sankatane. "I must find and bring our people back again."

"His home," she replied, "is on the top of the highest hill, but do not dare to go near him. What could a child like you do against such a wicked monster?"

"I'm going!" cried Sankatane.

His mother wept, "We are the only living creatures left in this vast and hilly land. If he should take you, who is left for me?"

But her son pushed her aside, saying, "Give me my father's spear, his knife, and his fire-stone. It must never be said that his son is weak. I shall kill the killer of our people. Only then will I return to you."

He left her in tears, and climbed the hills with courage, until at last he reached the highest hill of all. There on its summit he saw the monster Kholumolumo, huge beyond his wildest dreams, its belly bulging with all it had eaten. Silently and stealthily he crept towards it, with his father's spear poised to strike. Then he drove the blade into the creature's side.

Immediately there was a cry from inside the beast. Someone said, "Ow! Don't strike on this side, for we are still alive inside."

"They are alive!" cried Sankatane joyfully. So he crept around to the other side of the monster, and he thrust in his spear again. This time, out of the wound came the bleat of a goat in pain. He drove his spear in once again, nearer to the tail, to be greeted by the yelp of a dog, and he realised that it was pointless to continue to use his spear for he would only harm those inside.

The boy then walked round in front of the creature's mouth, in the hope of getting inside it and, as he had wanted, Kholumolumo opened his jaws and swallowed him. Once inside, he took his father's knife, and cut away the monster's heart and liver. Then with his father's flint he made a fire, and as the liver burned Kholumolumo died.

Sankatane then cut his way out of the huge monster, and freed all those inside. There was great rejoicing as they gained the open air, and one by one they asked, "Who has set us free?"

"I have set you free!" said Sankatane.

"This is the man to be our chief" they cried, and they agreed to make him chief of all the land. Upon the hilltop, beside the remains of the monster Kholumolumo, they built a village in gratitude to their new chief Sankatane.

For a while, life was happy for them all. Eventually jealousy broke out among them. Some said, "How is it that a child should be our chief, above the elders?" Then they planned to kill Sankatane, forgetting what they owed him.

But Sankatane guessed how they planned to surprise him by night, bind him and throw him over a cliff onto the rocks below. Silently they waited in the dark beside the pathway by the cliff, knowing that their chief would have to pass that way.

On that particular night, however, Sankatane changed huts with someone else, and when the murderers saw the other man approach along the path, they seized him and threw him onto the rocks below. So he died. The next day when the murderers saw their chief walking among his people, they realised that they had killed the wrong man. He called the culprits to him and asked, "Why have you killed one of my men?" They had no answer for him.

Again they tried, and this time they hid a man in a sheaf of sugar cane, bound loosely round, and left leaning against the wall of his hut, so that when their chief went inside the hut, the hidden man could stab him. But the man that Sankatane sent to fetch fire to light his pipe was stabbed instead, and again the wrong man died.

At last the warriors said among themselves, "It is pointless to try to kill our chief by night. The darkness is on his side. Tomorrow, when the sun is high, and we can see his face, we will end his life. Then we will rule instead."

On the following day, Sankatane called his mother to him and said, "I will try to escape my fate no longer. I will let them murder me, but tell them this. Those who kill me, will in turn be killed. Each will kill the other. They will fight each other to be chief. Plagues will kill man and beast, and they will live to regret what they are planning now."

When the sun had reached the highest point in the heavens; he watched with sorrow as they came to strangle him, and he did not try to stop them. And so, at last he died.

Before long had passed, Sankatane's prophesy came true. The men who had plotted against his life, now plotted against each other, until not one was left. It was many years and many generations before peace and fellowship returned to Lesotho instead of the sorrow and trouble brought about by the monster Kholumolumo.

THE LIFTING OF THE CURSE

LESOTHO

Maliepetsane was a little orphan girl who lived with her aunt and uncle. After they had given her a home for many years, they decided that it was time to receive some payment for their care. Perhaps there was someone with lobola to offer – a generous marriage price for such a pretty bride?

Now, far away from this orphan girl, there lived a couple who had an only son. A tragedy had fallen on the home when he was born, for an evil spirit had bewitched him: the top of his body was that of man, while from his waist downwards was the long, thin cold-blooded scaly body of a snake.

"If you want him to stay with any human parts at all," laughed the evil spirit, "you must always imitate the crowing of a cock when you speak to him. And no human must ever see him except yourselves."

The parents loved their only child so dearly that they obeyed the evil one's instructions exactly. The boy grew to manhood without ever seeing another human being. His parents provided him with every comfort, and in order that he could rest at ease, they had built a shelf for him against the wall inside his hut – and there he lay day in, day out, with his long reptile tail trailing on the ground.

Eventually, he begged his parents for a wife, to bring some change to his life. Just then it happened that they heard of the orphan-girl Maliepetsane, and they felt that surely this was an opportunity for their strange son. A girl with neither father nor mother was all that could be desired, for what would her guardians care for her husband's looks, so long as they received a good bride-price for the orphan?

Arrangements were quickly made, and Maliepetsane was fetched to her bridegroom's home. There she was told that never was she to set eyes upon her husband, and that when she talked to him, or took food to his hut, she was to crow like a cock before she set it down beside the door.

Although it sounded most unusual, she was an obedient girl, and for a long time she did as she had been told. She cooked his food for him, saw to his needs, and held long conversations with him through his tightly closed door. Eventually, however, curiosity got the better of her and she said to herself, "What sort of man have I married? Why can't I see his face?" Finally

her desire to see him became so great that she decided to disobey her orders.

When next her husband's parents went to gather mealies from the field and she was left alone, Maliepetsane went to her husband's hut, and spoke boldly through the door without first giving the usual "crow". "It is I, your wife, Maliepetsane. Let me in. It is time we saw each other." There was no reply, so she carefully parted the thatch to peep inside, and there she saw her husband, lying on a shelf, with his long and scaly tail trailing on the ground! He looked up with startled eyes as Maliepetsane, with a scream of fear, turned and ran wildly all the long way to the home of her aunt and uncle.

As quickly as he could, her bridegroom reached the ground, and slithered down the path to catch her. But the evil spell was already working. Gradually his arms shrank, and all his features changed to those of a full-bodied and enormous snake.

Deeply unhappy, he now made for the waters of a nearby lake, and plunged into it to hide his reptile shape from the world. In that way he returned to where his kind belonged.

When his parents came back and found his empty hut, with both he and Maliepetsane gone, they guessed what had taken place, and were overcome with grief. They hastily fetched their herd of lovely cows and took them to the lake as an offering to the crocodile that lived there. Perhaps his power would help them in their sorrow.

They drove the cows to the water's edge, and one by one they urged them in – and one by one the crocodile came up to eat them. As the last cow disappeared, the giant crocodile licked his lips, and crawled out upon the bank and looked at the two humans weeping on the shore.

He gazed at them in silence for a while, then he turned and swam beneath the surface of the water. When he returned, the bridegroom snake was with him. The two creatures climbed the river bank and then suddenly the crocodile turned and tore the reptile skin of the mighty snake from head to tail. Out of it stepped the handsome human form of a strong young man. The dreadful curse was lifted, and the bridegroom was free to walk on his own two legs for the first time in his life! Needless to say, his first journey was to the village of his wife's guardians, to claim his bride.

There was rejoicing and thanksgiving when he arrived there – for Maliepetsane was quite convinced she had married a snake! All ended as it should, for the two of them enjoyed long years of happiness together among their children and their children's children.

SEETEETELANE AND THE EGG-CHILD

LESOTHO

Seeteetelane and his blind old mother were so desperately poor that even their clothes and food had to come from the cane rats in the nearby river banks. From day to day the boy trapped these little creatures, and back at home he would skin and cook them for their supper. Then he would sew the little skins together into coverings, and that was all they had for warmth in the bitter cold of the winter nights.

If he had been lucky in his hunt, there would be breakfast for the morning, but if the catch had been a small one, he and his mother would go hungry.

Being blind, his mother was of little help to him, for she could not even gather wood, let alone do any cooking. It was therefore a hard life for the young boy, and little pleasure came his way. However, he took it all good-naturedly, and never complained.

One day when he returned from hunting, he stopped in surprise, for there laid out upon the floor of his mother's hut, was a delicious meal. All their favourite foods and, joy of joys, no rat meat! He turned to his mother who was sitting in the shadows and said, "Mother, who brought this meal? And how did you manage to cook it?"

"Son," she replied, "how, with my sightless eyes, could I see who came in and out? I have seen and heard nothing."

So they ate heartily and slept equally well, thanking in their hearts whoever had provided their feast. And the next day Seeteetelane went back to the river to hunt for cane rats. Luck was against him this time, and he came back empty-handed.

As he went into his mother's hut to warn her that they would be hungry that night, he felt behind the door where the wood was kept, for some kindling to start a fire. However, instead of feeling wood, he put his hand on something smooth and round. He jumped with fright, thinking he had touched a snake.

But he was wrong, for it was a large ostrich egg. "Oh!" he exclaimed to the egg, "where did you come from?" Here at least was something to eat for their evening meal.

He was about to pick it up and take it to his mother when it cracked in two, and out stepped a girl, more beautiful than any he had ever seen. She smiled and said, "Because you have

80

always been a good and dutiful son to your blind old mother, I am going to help you – but there is a condition to my help. You must never, never, never let anyone know that I am an Egg-Child. If you want help from me, you must guard your tongue."

Of course he promised faithfully. She disappeared and was soon back again with plenty of clothes and food. Time went on happily. The Egg-Child lived with them, and day after day she fed and clothed Seeteetelane and his mother by her magic, until the boy started to take all her help for granted. It sometimes happens that those who have everything done for them, lose the wish to work, and do nothing in return. Seeteetelane became just like that. Now that the food came easily, there was no point in going out to trap rats. So he never set any more traps. He no longer sat by the fire in the evenings, softening rat skins to make a warm winter covering. All things came without any effort, provided by the lovely girl from the magic egg. He accepted them as his right.

His idle thoughts now turned to his uncle who lived nearby. He began a habit of visiting his uncle's village, where the dancing and the merrymaking continued all through the night. He returned to his blind and lonely old mother later and later, until one night, being too drunk to think what words he used, he called out loudly as he reached the door, "Where is the Egg-Child, and why is she not here to welcome me home?"

"What did you call me?" answered the girl from inside the hut. "You have broken your promise. Tomorrow you eat rat meat once more, and clothe yourself in rat skins!" While Seeteetelane slept that night, she gathered all the things that she had brought to the hut and disappeared, leaving him as poor as he had ever been.

Throughout the winter days and nights that followed, Seeteetelane and his mother hungered and shivered in the cold. Bitterly he regretted his broken promise to the lovely girl. One day he wept out loud, "The girl who was my friend has deserted us! How can I continue without her?"

His mother scolded him, "Your broken promise made her go. It's all your fault. See the trouble that your stupidity has brought upon us both!"

Realising his foolishness at last, he made a promise to himself that he would never be tempted to visit his uncle's village again. He kept that promise faithfully for many months. And he went back to his rat-hunting as in the past.

One day while he was out hunting, a flock of birds flew into his mother's hut, bringing food with them. They swept the floor, and tidied all round. Then, making up the fire, they cooked a delicious meal. When Seeteetelane came back that evening, tired and hungry, he rejoiced to find a feast, once more, spread out upon the floor.

"Mother," he said to the old woman, "who has done this?"

"How should I know?" she answered, "for I cannot see. All I heard was the soft fluttering of wings."

They ate the food with joy, and slept that night with fresh blessings on the unknown giver of the food.

Seeteetelane was determined not to be lazy this second time, so went away as usual to hunt at the riverside. Again the same flock of birds came during his absence. This time they brought firewood as well as food, and this was more than welcome, for there was little fuel to be found on the bare hills around.

Again, on his return, Seeteetelane asked his mother who, she thought, was responsible for this kindness. "How should I know?" she answered. "Hide behind the door and see for yourself."

Next day he followed his mother's advice, and before he had been hiding long he heard the whirring of many wings, and the flock of little birds came into the hut as before. They swept the floor, and laid the fire ready to cook the food that they had brought. When the feast was ready they prepared to leave.

But before they had time to reach the door, Seeteetelane jumped from his hiding place, and closed it firmly on them.

The hut was straightaway filled with fluttering shapes, and in a flash the birds had disappeared while in their place appeared the same lovely girl who had helped him before. Now that he had found her again, Seeteetelane begged her to stay with him forever as his wife. The girl agreed, but made the same condition as before.

Once more she supplied their wants by her magic, and Seeteetelane kept his promise. But after some time had passed, his wife decided that she wanted to test him, so she asked to be taken to meet the uncle in whose company he had been so foolish in the past.

The path to his uncle's village was now overgrown with weeds from lack of use. But when they reached the river, she told him to go on alone and bring his uncle to her. Before they parted she said to him, "Don't start talking or you'll be tempted to stay once more – and you might forget me!"

So Seeteetelane went on into the village, looking for his uncle. At first he took no notice of his old companions, who begged him to stay. But soon they had persuaded him to join them for just one drink of his uncle's famous beer, and in no time he had forgotten all about his wife waiting for him at the riverside.

The evening came and then the night, and after making merry, Seeteetelane slept in his uncle's hut. All through the night his wife waited, and early in the morning a neighbour saw her. "Who are you?" he asked, "and what are you doing here alone?"

"I have waited all night for my husband Seeteetelane," she answered. "He has forgotten me while he celebrates with bad companions in his uncle's hut."

The neighbour took her to the uncle and said, "This is the wife who your nephew has left alone at the riverside all through the night."

Even the uncle was horrified at such behaviour, but when he woke, Seeteetelane didn't remember the hard lesson he had once learned. "Oh, don't worry about her!" he yawned. "She is only an Egg-Child. She came out of an ostrich egg!"

"You have broken your word for the last time," said his wife, breaking in. "I can trust you no longer. This time I will go for ever!"

True to her word she disappeared, never to return, leaving Seeteetelane and his mother to live once more on cane rats, and in the greatest poverty, to the end of their days.

Narrator: Melesala Khan

THAKANE

LESOTHO

Long, long ago, in the land now called Lesotho, there lived a man, his wife and five daughters. Thakane, the eldest, was lovely beyond imagining, and those who met her were charmed not only by her beauty, but by her gracious ways as well. However, she was as silent as she was lovely, and of the many suitors who had come hoping to marry her, not one had succeeded in persuading Thakane to talk. "What use is a wife who will not talk?" they asked, and she remained at home, still unmarried.

However, Masilo and Ntho, two close friends, were so attracted by her that they were determined that one of them would win her hand. So, when her father announced that he would give her to the man who first made her speak, these two youths came forward to try.

"May my blessing go with you," said the father, "for I am weary of my daughter's stubborn silence."

The boys found Thakane hoeing out the weeds in her mother's mabele field and, without a word, they joined her, hoeing at her side. Carefully Ntho turned the sods and tilled the ground, but Masilo pulled up the mabele plants one by one, and re-planted them upside down. He went on doing this for quite a while, while Thakane took no notice of him. But at last, she couldn't bear it any longer. He was ruining the whole crop. So she burst out, "You fool! What do you imagine you are doing?"

"She has spoken! She has spoken!" cried Masilo, rushing to the girl's father with the good news. As Masilo's own father was a powerful chief, there was great rejoicing in Thakane's family when they heard that such an important young man had won the silent beauty's hand. But day after day Thakane hid in her mother's hut, refusing to admit that she had been tricked into breaking her silence. So disappointed and frustrated, the two friends went home.

However, they were unable to forget the lovely, silent girl, so they came back and built two huts from which they could watch her from time to time.

As the months wore on, and the crops ripened, platforms were built from which the village children scared away the birds that came to eat the grain. One day, while Thakane was taking her turn at this task, Masilo and Ntho joined her and took over the work of chasing away the destructive birds. All through the scorching day the two of them watched the fields for her.

Neither of them said a word to her until, dry with thirst as the afternoon lengthened, Ntho asked for a melon from the adjoining field. Now, this particular field belonged to Thakane's mother, and the melons were ripe and juicy. There was one melon of wondrous size and sweetness, and this one in particular the old woman prized beyond all the others. Her children knew that to touch it would anger her beyond words.

Risking her mother's rage, Thakane picked the wonder-melon and handing it to Ntho said, "Only this, among all my mother's fruits, is good enough for you. I am ready, and willing to be your wife."

Ntho could hardly believe his good fortune, but before he had time to thank her, Thakane's mother came to the field to pick her precious melon. Unable to find it, she called to Thakane to find what had become of it. There was no reply, and the old woman became very angry.

When the two youths realised that there was trouble on the way, they took refuge in one of the huts that they had built. Thakane, knowing only too well the power of her mother's anger, called up the water from the river. Up, up, up it rose until it had formed a lake around them, which finally swallowed them, huts and all.

Thakane then ran into the water to join her chosen husband, and so escaped the lashing of her mother's tongue. As she did so, one of her sisters saw her sink beneath the water. "Father," the sister cried, "Thakane, our sister, has drowned herself, all because of our mother's anger!"

In despair, her father called his friends, and together they searched the water that had appeared so mysteriously, but no trace of either the huts or the girl could they find. Hour after hour the old man sat at the water's edge, sadly lamenting the loss of his lovely daughter, when unexpectedly, the water began to dry up before his very eyes, bringing the two huts to view again.

There the father found Masilo, Ntho and Thakane, laughing and talking as though nothing had happened. Seeing the look of happiness on the face of his strange and lovely daughter, he smiled with satisfaction and quietly went away.

But Thakane's troubles were by no means at an end for, on the following morning the two youths decided to return to their parents' village to make arrangements for the wedding feast. Telling Thakane to await their return, they left her. The girl begged them not to start the festivities before returning for her, in case with all the fun and laughter, they forgot to come back.

She was right in her worry because Masilo and Ntho danced for many days without once remembering their promise. Thakane grieved day after day but, still afraid of her mother's anger she had no desire to return home. Eventually she decided to follow the two young men, and before long reached the river where the village women drew their daily water.

She waited sorrowfully on the bank for some hours, and at last slid beneath the surface of one of the deep crystal-clear pools, hoping that, if anyone saw her under the water, they would spread the news. She hoped this would remind Masilo and Ntho of their forgotten promise that they would return to her.

All through the morning Thakane waited beneath the water, and at midday a grizzled old woman came to draw water for her chief. Stooping to fill her gourd she saw a beautiful face looking up at her from the depths, and thought it was a reflection of her own. "What is this?" she exclaimed excitedly. "How have I become so beautiful? Surely with such beauty, I have no need to do a servant's work? I will leave such to the plain and ugly!" So she returned to the village very pleased with herself, and sat in the sun for the rest of the day. But no one came to help Thakane.

When the beer-pots were finally empty, Masilo and Ntho remembered the reason for their visit. Highly ashamed, they hastened back to Thakane, but as they crossed the river at the village pool, they were astonished to see her lovely face looking reproachfully up at them from its depths. The two young men begged for her forgiveness and, being kind, she forgave them.

When the wedding ceremonies were over and Thakane's relatives had returned to their homes, Ntho and his wife settled down happily and the young bride cheerfully hoed and tended her mother-in-law's crops each day as a daughter-in-law should do.

One day on her way back from the fields, Thakane met a strange-looking girl who was completely naked except for a torn and scanty goatskin which she clutched about her ugly body. "Have pity, kind stranger!" sobbed the girl. "My clothes were stolen by a wicked thief, and I am a long, long way from my home. Please lend me your clothes until I can find some for myself."

Although Thakane was a tender-hearted girl, she was far too modest to go naked herself, so she refused the stranger's request. At this the girl wept louder than ever, "May your husband's cattle increase by hundreds if you will only lend me your clothes for a while. As a reward for your goodness I will provide the most luscious grazing for your husband's herds!"

"Well," thought Thakane, "a short while without my clothes seems to promise the reward of good pastures!" So, taking off her clothes, she handed them to the stranger and hid in a hut nearby.

When a long time had passed and the clothes had still not been returned, Thakane draped some creepers about her naked body and went to look for the ugly stranger. Eventually she found the girl, who refused to return Thakane's clothes and said, "Let me wear them a little while longer, and in return I will provide your husband with a fine hut for his chickens!"

Before she had time to argue, the stranger had disappeared and Thakane crept back into the deserted hut. She was so ashamed of her nakedness that she asked the earthen floor to swallow her. This the floor obligingly did, covering up her shame. Let's leave poor Thakane there for a while.

This was by no means the end of the stranger's mischief for, having disguised her body in Thakane's clothes, she now disguised her face to look like Thakane. Even Ntho was deceived.

But although she tricked Ntho, Masilo was clever enough to see through the disguise and on the following day told Ntho's mother.

"Ah!" whispered the mother, "it seems as though the evil one, 'Tail-of-a-dog' is at her tricks again." Tail-of-a-dog was a troublesome woman who had been born with a dog's tail, and who travelled around bringing trouble to all. "We will set a trap for her," she decided, "which will trick this creature into showing whether she is a human or a dog."

They told Ntho of their suspicions, and although he did not believe them at first, he took a large stone and went to sit beside his so-called wife. As he pretended to stroke her, he dropped the stone against her. At once she wriggled away from him, and cried out, "Eeeeeh!"

"What hurt you, wife, to make you cry out like that?" Ntho asked, guessing that the stone had fallen on her dog's tail, hidden underneath her leather apron.

"Oh!" she replied, sidling away from him, "it was nothing but a sudden stomach-ache." However, Ntho was not satisfied, so on the following day he dug a deep trench beside his hut. Then, into the trench he poured quantities of milk. One by one he made the village women jump across the trench and, sure enough, when Tail-of-a-dog made her leap, down came the dog's tail and splashed in the milk. The onlookers all saw what had happened. Ntho grabbed the tell-tale "tail", and pulled the wicked creature into the trench. Quickly the villagers filled in the trench and so buried Tail-of-a-dog so that the country was freed for evermore from the wicked creature.

As the earth swallowed up his false wife, so it returned Ntho's true bride. Thakane came back to life from her earthly covering, and there was much singing and dancing as the girl was welcomed back to her husband's home. They lived happily together for ever after.

Narrator:
Melesala Khan

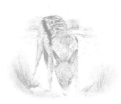

HOATITI AND THE GOAT THIEVES

LESOTHO

Hoatiti and his wife had a herd of beautiful goats. They were proud of these valuable animals, but one by one the goats were being killed and eaten. They were sure that Mpungushi, the wicked jackal, was the thief. So Hoatiti's wife decided to build a new and stronger kraal in which to keep them, with higher, stronger stone walls, so that nothing could break in and harm their precious herd.

All day long she toiled in the hot sun and when night came her work was finished. The new wall was tall and strong. She put the goats inside, closing the entrance firmly, then she and her husband settled down happily for the night. Their troubles must now be over, and they could rest in peace.

However, when she looked out of her hut door next morning, the woman saw, with great annoyance, that the wall was broken and many stones scattered on the ground. To their great surprise though, she and her husband found that the goats were unharmed, and none were missing.

Hoatiti studied the spoor on the ground carefully. "It is definitely the jackal who visited us last night," he informed his wife. "He is the one who has ruined your hard work."

"Well," said the woman with a sigh, "I will build the wall even higher and stronger." So she began to repair the damaged wall with more, and larger rocks. She finished just as the sun went down and, after putting the goats inside, she said to Hoatiti, "The goats should be safe tonight!" after which she went wearily to bed.

Early the following morning the woman again saw to her anger that, not only were the walls broken down, but to add insult to injury, Mpungushi the jackal was standing on one of the walls, laughing to himself. She called to her husband and he replied, "Wife, bring me my sling. I'll shoot the impudent creature."

Now, the jackal knew nothing about slings, and thought that he was perfectly safe at that distance. As he wanted to hear what Hoatiti and his wife were talking about, he pricked his ears forward to listen. Suddenly there was a sharp pain in his side and he raced off to the safety of the veld with all speed.

When he was a good way away, Mpungushi paused to examine himself. Like all jackals, he was most inquisitive. He had not seen the thing that had hurt him, for it had travelled too fast, so he said to himself, "That was very strange. I don't know what hurt me. It couldn't have been Hoatiti and his wife for they were far, far away. I must go back tonight and find out what really happened."

The jackal returned in the light of early dawn, so that when Hoatiti's wife looked out of her hut, she saw him for the second time, standing upon the broken wall. Again she called her husband, and again he told her to fetch his sling, adding, "This time I'll kill him."

Hoatiti chose a larger stone for his sling, took very careful aim and he sent the stone whizzing on its journey. It struck the jackal so hard that he jumped high in the air with a yelp of pain. Then off he rushed into the veld once more crying, "Woaw, woaw, woaw!"

On his headlong flight the jackal met Senonnori, who had never been one of his friends. "Mpungushi, why are you crying?" he asked.

"Crying?" snapped the jackal. "I'm not crying. I'm singing!"

But Senonnori did not believe him, and laughed, "Well, my friend, sing again. I want to hear you better!"

The jackal decided to get even with him later, and changed the subject as an idea came into his crafty head. "Do you know Hoatiti?" he asked pleasantly. Senonnori liked the creatures of the wilds to think that he knew everybody so he replied, "Of course I know him."

"Are you afraid of him?" asked the jackal.

"Afraid of him?" laughed Senonnori, "why, if I even look at him, he runs away."

"Splendid!" smirked the jackal. "Then, if you are as brave as all that will you come with me and chase him away? He is annoying me."

"Certainly, certainly," replied Senonnori. "Show me where he lives, and I will deal with him." Mpungushi took Senonnori to the goat kraal and told him to climb the wall if he wanted to see Hoatiti. "He is not expecting you," he added, "so you will have the advantage. I will hide behind the wall, because he is expecting me!"

Not long after this Hoatiti went to the door of his hut and, seeing another creature on the wall, called for his sling once more.

"Did you hear what that two-legged creature said?" whispered Mpungushi from his hiding place. "No," answered Senonnori excitedly, "what did he say?"

"He said," replied the jackal slyly, "what is that beautiful creature standing on the wall? Wife, come and admire him!"

Now, Senonnori was very vain, so he strutted boldly backwards and forwards along the top of the wall to show off his beauty.

Suddenly he felt a violent pain in his side, which made him stop. "What bit me?" he asked in surprise. "I didn't hear or see anything!" Then another stone hit him and, with a yell of pain he rushed to where the jackal was hiding.

"We will come again tomorrow," replied the jackal comfortingly, "because I don't know the answer either. There's something here that can bite from a distance. We must find out what it is."

The following day the two animals went again to the goat kraal, and when Senonnori climbed onto the wall, Hoatiti was waiting for him. The stone that came whistling from the sling struck its target with such force that it knocked Senonnori right off the wall, and he scuttled away into the veld crying, "Weee, weee, weed"

The jackal doubled up with laughter, and called after him, "My friend, if you are singing, can't you sing a bit louder. I can't hear you properly! Don't you realise that you can't beat Hoatiti? He is so clever, that he can bite you from far away!"

However, Senonnori was a brave little creature, and he was also very, very angry. "I will go again tomorrow," he said, "and I will kill this one who bites from far away."

True to his words, Senonnori was on the wall as the sun rose the following morning and, when the first stone hit him, he jumped down and bravely attacked Hoatiti. But Hoatiti was prepared for this, and the next stone was fired at such a short range, that it knocked Senonnori head over heels. He was only just able to escape.

"We must kill this creature," said Hoatiti to his wife, "for this is the one who has been killing our goats."

Hoatiti and his wife decided to make friends with the jackal, and they offered him a reward of a fat goat if he would help them kill Senonnori. "When this is done," added Hoatiti to his wife, "we will kill Mpungushi too. In that way we can get rid of both of them."

The jackal agreed to help, but on one condition. "First you must give me the goat," he insisted, "so that I can use it to bait the trap."

Hoatiti did not trust the jackal, so he killed the goat and poisoned the flesh, in the hope of killing both of them.

Later in the day Mpungushi went to see Senonnori, and pretended to be most sorry for him. "My friend," he sympathised, "your wounds have made you ill. I have stolen a goat from Hoatiti. Let's have a feast together, you and I. Come, I will help you to my hut."

Senonnori leaned upon the jackal's shoulder and together they went to Mpungushi's home, where they sat down under the branches of a tree and built a fire on which to roast the goat. After chatting for a while, the jackal began to make a fuss of Senonnori, stroking his arms and legs, and running his claws through the creature's hair in a most affectionate manner. Gradually the paw that was stroking Senonnori went higher, and closer to his friend's neck and, just as Senonnori had decided what a dear, sympathetic friend he was fortunate enough to have, Mpungushi slipped a noose around Senonnori's neck, and hauled him up to the branch above.

There the treacherous jackal left Senonnori, while he hurried to fetch Hoatiti, shouting, "Come, Hoatiti, I have caught the thief who has been stealing your goats. If you are quick, you can help me to kill him!"

Together Hoatiti and Mpungushi built a big fire, using green branches, so that the thick smoke soon suffocated Senonnori. As soon as he was dead, the jackal invited all his jackal friends – and together they sat down to enjoy their feast of goat flesh.

There is no need to tell you what happened then, for you will remember that Hoatiti had poisoned the meat. Hoatiti and his wife were soon rid of the goat thieves for evermore.

Narrator: Melesala Khan

THE STORY OF FUDWAZANA AND GONGONGO

XHOSA

When this great big world was a very much kinder place than it is today, all the animals lived in friendship. They had no fear of one another. They lived happily together, ruled by the great and noble King of Beasts, Lord Lion.

The natural food of these creatures was vegetables and greens, the same as human beings eat. But because the animals had had no land given to them by the Creator when he divided up the earth, they were forced to live by taking what they could from the cultivated lands of their human neighbours. This was dangerous, and many were caught and killed. The loss of so many of his subjects was a great sorrow to King Lion – so much so that he called a meeting of his people.

Now, the lion was by no means the largest of the creatures of the wilds. Many were very much larger – for instance his Chief Councillor the elephant, the rhinoceros, the tall giraffe and others. He was looked up to for his justness and for his bravery against the humans whose fields they robbed. So because of the praise that his devoted subjects gave him, and also because he had no rival, Lord Lion had grown to think that there was no one on earth so powerful as he.

But when the lion considered that he was the only lord of the earth, he had overlooked Gongongo, a huge monster which ranged the country far beyond the lion's kingdom. He lived on whatever he could find – even greens, when he could find no flesh. He was so enormous that he did not even chew small animals like sheep and goats, but swallowed them whole. He could easily take three of these little creatures at a time into his enormous belly. And of course he did not attend the meeting which Lord Lion had summoned.

"My subjects!" their king solemnly addressed his people when they all were gathered together.

"Too many animals are being killed as they visit the gardens of our human neighbours. We must cultivate some gardens of our own. Let each animal hoe and till his own small patch, where he can grow the food he needs to eat. Come, let us begin the search for a suitable place."

There was an excited hum of agreement amongst the animals as they discussed their ruler's plan. "Why shouldn't we grow our own crops?" they asked each other. And so the search began. First one piece of land was examined, and then another – until at last they discovered a broad fertile plain far away from any human beings, which pleased them all.

On the following morning the king provided each animal with a hoe and all was bustle and excitement as they dug, scraped and tilled to get their gardens planted.

The land that they had chosen was rich and fertile, and soon grew good crops, so that the animals went happily each day to reap the reward of their labours. Imagine their surprise and anger when they went as usual one day to gather their daily food, and found that the whole area had been laid bare. Not a blade nor a leaf of all that they had planted was to be found, while in the very centre of the field squatted the most enormous creature that any of them had ever seen.

They fled back in terror and told their king of this disaster. So, advising them to remain behind, the lion went to punish the intruder. But when he saw how big it was, and how fierce it looked, Lord Lion realised that this enemy was far too big for him. Instead of fighting him he roared angrily, "Who are you? How dare you trespass on the land that my subjects have chosen to grow their crops? And what right have you to come into my kingdom?"

In a frightful voice the creature bellowed in reply, "'Tis I, Gongongo, the one who swallows buffaloes alive, horns and all. I could swallow you, little lion, without even blinking. As for what I am doing on your land, why, I came here because I was hungry, and who's going to stop me?"

The lion, in spite of his bravery, gave one terrified look at the dreadful monster, then turned tail and ran for his life. There was dismay among his subjects when they realised that even their highly respected king could do nothing to get rid of this danger.

After an uncomfortable period of silence, Fudwazana the tortoise shuffled forward and said, "My Lord Lion, I will rid you of this wicked monster, if you will provide me with a weapon. Give me a little axe that is small enough to hide beneath my shell; sharpen it well, and you will see that I am telling the truth."

Although he did not believe that so small a creature could possibly overcome the mighty monster, Lord Lion willingly gave the tortoise a well-sharpened axe. Quite a long time later, for the tortoise can't walk very fast, Fudwazana reached the field and waddled boldly up to the mountain of flesh. There he stopped and called out, "Who are you whose wretched body is making such a mess of our field?"

The creature replied as he had to the lion, "I am Gongongo, the one who swallows buffaloes with ease, horns and all! Three sheep at once are nothing to me. You, Fudwazana, are so small that I could toss you under my tongue and never think of you again!"

"Well, my friend," answered the tortoise, "I would be very grateful if you would do just that, because now that you have eaten all our food there is nothing left for us to eat. I would look upon it as a great privilege to live beneath your tongue for then, my lord, I could catch the odd scraps of the food you eat." Whereupon he waddled his way right up in front of Gongongo's mouth, and the enormous creature caught him and tossed him under his big yellow tongue.

"Ah!" chuckled Fudwazana to himself as the huge mouth closed over him, "now we will see who has the greater brain!" And pulling the little axe from under his shell, he began to chop at the base of Gongongo's leathery tongue.

Chop! chop! chop! The enormous creature sat up and shook his head, wondering what troubled him. Again chop! chop! chop! went the little razor-sharp axe, and this time Gongongo gave a thunderous roar of pain that was heard throughout the country. All the animals shivered with fear for they thought their dreaded enemy was coming to attack them. But Fudwazana was not wasting time and as soon as he reached the root of the creature's tongue, he chopped it right out.

The roars of pain grew fainter and fainter until, as the animals ran forward with shouts of encouragement to the tortoise, the noise ceased altogether, and they realised that Fudwazana had carried out his promise.

When they reached the field they found their enemy dying, and the triumphant tortoise climbing out of its enormous mouth singing loudly,

"'Tis I, 'tis I, the Tortoise, 'tis I, who has killed Gongongo."

Needless to say, the animals made a tremendous fuss of the brave Fudwazana. They carried him home with shouts of joy and songs of praise. For ever after they were able to grow their crops in peace and safety. Ever since that day tortoises have been respected by all the creatures of the wilds. They consider they are the wisest as well as the most cunning, brave and persevering animals of them all. Hurray for Tortoises!

Narrator: Thandiwe Mceleni

THE TWINS AND THE
CANNIBAL'S FEAST

LESOTHO

Reli and Relinyane were twin boys. Relinyane was clever, small and agile, while his twin brother Reli was clumsy and large and stupid. It was as though a Spirit of Stupidity lived inside him.

It was Relinyane's task each day to take his father's cattle out to graze and he used to take Reli with him, to prevent him worrying those at home. As Relinyane left their hut, he took with him a fire-pot with a glowing ember from his mother's fire.

Each time they arrived at the grazing ground, the small twin sat the large twin beneath a shady tree and built a little fire. Then, telling Reli to watch the cattle and look after the fire, Relinyane went to trap mice and birds to cook for their midday meal. Later, he would have to feed his brother, for he was too stupid to feed himself.

In the evenings, when they took the cattle home, Relinyane would guide Reli to his mother's hut, then count his father's cattle before he closed the entrance to the kraal. After this, he fetched their evening meal, and again he had to feed his twin. All this goes to show how much Reli relied upon Relinyane.

One day, when as usual they took the cattle out to pasture, Relinyane forgot to take his little fire pot. This was indeed unfortunate, because he was hungrier than ever that day, and had no wish to eat raw mice. So he made a plan. "Brother," he said, "don't leave this place while I am away. I'm going to fetch some fire from the cannibal's hut across the river. If he sees me and chases me, you will never run fast enough to escape so you must ask the earth to swallow you. Now, say this after me. 'Earth, earth, please open and swallow me!'" Three times Relinyane made Reli repeat these magic words after him, then he sat Reli down under a tall ironwood tree while he left for the cannibal's hut, to steal some fire.

When he arrived at the hut, Relinyane found an ugly old woman cooking a pot of corn-gruel outside her doorway. He knew she was a cannibal, probably the grandmother of many cannibals, but all the same it was wisest to be polite. So he said, "Good morning to you, grandmother." The old woman was very deaf, so she asked the boy what he had said. "I said: 'Good morning to you, grandmother'," repeated Relinyane, "I have come to ask for some fire."

The old woman, who was almost as blind as she was deaf, thought it was her grandchild speaking, so she answered good-naturedly, "Child of my child, of course you may have some of the fire, but first help me scoop this gruel to the pot inside the hut, for I am preparing your father's beer."

"Very well," replied Relinyane, taking the first brimming measure into the hut to her. Several times he carried the scoop to her as instructed, and between each trip he built up the fire, until the gruel boiled and bubbled fiercely in the big pot.

"Eh!" croaked the old woman, "you are making the gruel too hot; it has already been cooked." "Oh no!" replied the boy, "it still smells raw."

And as she bent forward to sniff, he threw the contents of the scoop into her face, hoping to rid the land of one more cannibal.

With the scalding gruel blinding her completely now, the old woman screamed, "The child of my child is killing me!" Hearing her cries, her cannibal son came hurrying from the field to help and when he saw Relinyane running for his life, he gave chase. But fortunately for the boy, the cannibal was a fat man, and Relinyane was far ahead of him by the time he reached the tree under which he had left his stupid brother.

As he ran, Relinyane shouted, "Reli, the cannibal is coming. Remember what I told you!" "What did you tell me to do?" mumbled his twin. "If you told me to blow my nose, then I've just done so."

"You fool!" scolded Relinyane as he lost patience and boxed his brother's ears. "Ask the earth to swallow you, and be quick about it, or you will be eaten!" Then he lost no time in climbing up to the topmost branches of the tree.

Slowly Reli mumbled the magic words, and equally slowly the earth opened up in front of him, so that there was only just time for him to tumble into the crack before the cannibal came in sight. Reli pulled his loin-cloth in after him, but was not quite quick enough, for the crack closed on the cloth, leaving the one end of it above the earth.

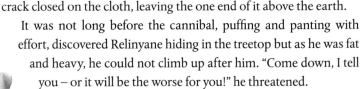

It was not long before the cannibal, puffing and panting with effort, discovered Relinyane hiding in the treetop but as he was fat and heavy, he could not climb up after him. "Come down, I tell you – or it will be the worse for you!" he threatened.

"First chop down the tree, and I will come down with it," replied Relinyane rudely. He was alarmed when the cannibal, without bothering to answer, took a small axe from his loin-strap, and began to chop at the trunk of the ironwood tree with all his strength.

Soon the sound of axe on wood echoed through the

countryside, but the ironwood tree was as hard as iron indeed, and the axe was soon too blunt to make even a mark upon it. Presently the cannibal gave up in disgust, and put down the axe to take a rest. It was then that he caught sight of Reli's loin-cloth peeping out of the crack in the earth. "Ah!" he cried greedily, "another one is hiding here. The earth will be easier to chop than this tree." Soon he was dragging poor Reli from his hiding place. He quickly slung him over one of his massive shoulders, and turned to take him home to eat.

"No, no, no!" begged Reli. "Please don't take me from my twin. Please eat me here."

"Very well," agreed the cannibal. "It will be a good punishment for your brother, to watch me enjoy my meal." So he built a large fire, killed Reli, cooked him and ate him.

"Will you leave the bones for me?" called Relinyane from the top of the tree. The cannibal did, as he had eaten quite enough, and he went home well satisfied with his enormous meal.

As soon as he was safely out of sight, Relinyane climbed down from the tree, spread his brother's loin-cloth upon the ground, carefully arranged the bones on it in their correct order. Then he folded the sides of the cloth over the bones, and chanted,

> "Reli, Reli, help your twin,
> Whose heart is full of fear.
> Come and drive the cattle home –
> The night will soon be here."

Slowly, the bones gathered new flesh round them, and gradually the boy came back to life. Reli lifted himself sleepily from the ground. Then, drawing a hand across his eyes, as though he had just awakened from a dream, he said, "Brother, how did I sleep so long? Our father will beat us if we lose his cows."

Relinyane replied, "Our father cannot beat you, because there is no you." Then he told Reli how the cannibal had caught and eaten him, and how he, Relinyane, had brought his twin back to life by magic.

After that, things changed a lot. When the boys reached their home that night, it was Reli who counted and put away his father's cows; it was Reli who fetched the evening meal; and it was Reli who did anything that required intelligence. The villagers were amazed. Soon everyone began to realise that Reli was as clever as his twin Relinyane.

Needless to say, though everyone wondered how this miracle had come about, the boys kept the secret to themselves. The twins lived happily and inseparably for many years, grateful to the wicked cannibal who had taken away the Spirit of Stupidity inside Reli's body by eating it!

Narrator: Melesala Khan

THE CROW AND THE JACKAL

LESOTHO

Though birds and beasts were not often friends together, even in the old days, it happened that mother crow and mother jackal came to visit each other often.

The crow had four fine fledgling chicks of which she was very proud, but the jackal had no children. She often complained about this to her feathered friend. In fact, she went on in this way so many times that one day she said to the crow, "My good friend, your children have reached the age when they are a nuisance to you. They are too young to fly with you to your feeding grounds, and too old for you to leave unattended in your hut. They could wander off and get into all kinds of danger. You know that I hunt by night, so I have plenty of spare time during the day. Won't you let me guard your children through the daylight hours?" The jackal's eyes glinted, and she hid a secret smile.

"That is indeed good of you," replied mother crow with gratitude. "I know that I can safely leave my little ones with you."

On the following day the crow flew light-heartedly to the feeding grounds leaving the jackal in charge of her four chicks. But as soon as she was out of sight, the jackal tempted one of the young crows out of the hut and, closing the door upon the other three, she killed and ate it.

The mother crow came back late that night, her crop bulging with food for her four children. She thanked the jackal for all she had done, but mother jackal said, "Do let me stay a little longer. I could help you to feed the little darlings." Then she added slyly, "One can never have too much of a good thing. I have thoroughly enjoyed my day."

The crafty creature went into the hut and brought out one of the little crows. The mother shared the contents of her crop between the fledglings as they were brought to her one by one, the jackal taking each one back when it had been fed.

As there were only three chicks left, the jackal brought the first little fledgling back again to the mother who thought it was her fourth child and gave it a second share of food. Imagining that all was well, the mother crow flew up into the tree, tucked her head under her wing, and was soon asleep.

On the following day the same thing happened. The wicked jackal cooked another meal for herself from one of the crow's children, so there were only two to be fed when the mother came home. But young crows are even greedier than most other little birds, and they were only too happy to eat a second helping from their mother's crop. So again the crow went to bed in the treetop, satisfied that she had attended to all four of her children.

On the third day the jackal made a tasty midday meal from another little crow, which left only one. Of course this remaining chick was satisfied after it had been brought back for the second time, so the jackal said to the mother crow, "I fed your children today myself. That's why only two of them are hungry. The other two are sleeping." And the mother crow believed her.

The fourth day saw the jackal making her midday meal off the last of the four fledglings and then the wicked creature disappeared into the forest. When the mother came home that night she found the hut empty, and realised the trick that had been played on her.

For many days the broken-hearted bird mourned the loss of her fledglings. Then, remembering that there was a human village nearby, where many little children played, she flew there, hoping that the sight would bring her comfort.

But the more she looked at other people's children, the more she longed to have one, or more than one, to take the place of her lost fledglings. One day, seeing a woman leave her twins unguarded while she hoed the mealie lands, the mother crow swooped down and stole first one, and then the other.

When Liloane, the mother, discovered that her little Ntjelo and Ntjelozana had disappeared, she ran to her husband and told him of their loss. But, instead of sympathising with her, the husband was very angry indeed, and told her that she should not have left the children alone. Unless she found them, he told her firmly, he would drive her from their home.

The broken-hearted woman asked her sister-in-law to help her to look for the babies, and together they left the village, not knowing where to go. All through the countryside they wandered, without finding any news of the missing twins. Each time that they returned empty-handed, the hard-hearted husband told her to go away and go on searching.

Day after day the two women wandered, until they found themselves farther from their homes than they had ever been before. As the midday heat beat down mercilessly upon them, they passed a youth herding his father's cows. The lad listened to the sorrowful song that Liloane sang as she walked along, until finally he called after them, "Sisters, why are you weeping?"

"We weep for my little ones, who have been stolen away from their home," sobbed Liloane. "If you want to find them," advised the boy, "follow the big black crow. Twice I saw her fly overhead towards the hills, and each time she carried a little child. Travel westwards, and you will find them."

With their hopes renewed, the two women hastened on towards the setting sun. Liloane made up a new song:

> *"Ntjelo and Ntjelozana,*
> *Stolen by the big black crow;*
> *Answer my song my little ones,*
> *That I may know where to go."*

The two women had been walking for some hours, and were beginning to wonder if they would ever find the children, when they came to a village and heard an answer to the song. There they found the twins being cared for by the big black crow. When Liloane called her children by name, the bird could not stop them from running to their mother.

Overjoyed, Liloane went to the chief of the village to request the return of her children, but he replied, "How can I take the twins from the mother crow, when she says they belong to her?"

"They are mine! They are mine!" croaked the crow. "They are my very own flesh and blood!"

"She lies, the wicked bird," cried the women of the village. "These little ones are human, for they know their mother's voice. Look at them clinging to her now!"

The chief was so angry with the crow for her theft and her lies, that he banished her from his kingdom for evermore.

Liloane and her sister-in-law carried Ntjelo and Ntjelozana back to their father's home in triumph. The mother was forgiven by her husband, and together they built a village of their own, where they soon gathered their friends and relations around them.

The twins grew and, when the time was ripe, Ntjelo became a much respected chief of a nearby village, while Ntjelozana was chosen to be the first and foremost wife of their dearly beloved chief. Her bride-price of many fine cows brought riches beyond their fondest hopes, to the girl's ageing parents.

Narrator: Melesala Khan

THE PYTHON'S BRIDE

MALAWI

This is a tale about a man, his wife and two daughters. They lived in Malawi when the country was suffering from a severe drought. Food was scarce for even those who worked hard in the fields, while the lazy ones, needless to say, were forced to live by their wits – or starve. Some caught fish from the nearby lake; others hunted the small creatures of the wilds, while others, again, took to stealing from their hardworking neighbours' gardens.

The father of the two girls in this story was one of these thieves. All day long this man sat lazily, caring little that his wife and children were starving. To keep his own stomach full, he crept from hut to hut during the night and stole whatever he could find: a chicken perhaps, fruit, or grain from well-tended gardens.

One night Ngosa, the elder child, feeling more hungry than usual, decided that if her father went out to steal food, it must be all right for her to try. So she crept from the hut to take some fruit from a neighbour's tree.

"Sister, what are you hiding under your blanket?" asked the younger child after their hardworking mother had left the hut at dawn on the following day, to hoe her crops.

"Hush!" whispered Ngosa, putting her finger to her lips. "Don't you dare wake our father. See, I have food to fill our empty stomachs," and she produced from beneath her blanket a bunch of ripe bananas.

Being extremely hungry, the younger child did not ask where they came from. Taking the fruit that she was offered, she ate it with glee: but she was a jealous child, and envious of her elder sister's beauty. Here, she thought, was an opportunity to get Ngosa into trouble. So, when her mother returned hot and tired from the mealie-lands at midday, the child took her aside and whispered, "Mother, if you will give me twice my share of food today, I will share a secret with you."

"What is it, daughter?" asked the mother crossly. "Here, eat your fill," and she handed the greedy child all that she had brought from the lands.

"Ngosa, my sister, steals from our neighbour's trees!" she whispered softly in her mother's ear. Now, although the mother knew where her husband went at night, she, herself, was an honest woman. She had no wish for her children to follow their father's bad example so, catching Ngosa, she beat her without mercy and drove her out into the veld. She wouldn't even allow her to sleep in her home that night.

Storm clouds had gathered throughout the day, and down came the rain, and down to the river rushed the storm water, carrying Ngosa with it. And as the rushing water washed her into the swiftly-flowing river, so Santo, the big, strong water python, came up from the depths of his silent pool and swallowed her.

He took her down into the depths and, when he had reached his underwater cave, he brought her out of his stomach unharmed. He made her welcome, and there, in his home, the huge snake married Ngosa.

Days of happiness followed for both the girl and her bridegroom, as the snake pressed both gifts and kindness upon his bride: beaded finery, clothes of the finest texture, possessions more wonderful than she had ever seen before.

The big snake even gave her a magic sleigh that shone with such dazzling brilliance that it was invisible to the human eye. Two enchanted oxen took the happy bride wherever she wanted to go.

"Take your magic sleigh," said Santo the python one day, "and visit your parents' home. It would be good for your mother to know that happiness and love has come to you." So the little outcast returned to the home of her childhood and, made invisible by the python's magic, she joined once more in the daily life she used to live. And the first night she arrived, she found that her father was as lazy as ever and still a thief.

On the following morning, when the village girls took their clay pots to draw water from the river, Ngosa went with them, although being still invisible, they could not see her. First they bathed, laughing and talking as they splashed each other in the clear, cool water. When they had tired of their fun, they filled their pots with water and in pairs they helped each other to lift the heavy water pots on to each other's head.

"Now," said the leader of the party, "two by two we will carry the water back," and in pairs they departed. Ngosa's little sister had no companion to go with her along the way so, when she reached her mother's hut she was crying – though she realised it was her own fault that she had lost her sister who used to pair with her.

At the sight of her sister's tears, the invisible Ngosa's heart was touched, so she lifted the heavy pot from the child's head, while the little girl looked around her in astonishment. She was more astonished still when she heard Ngosa say, "Little sister, I have come to tell you that I am now the wife of someone who is more kind to me than you could ever imagine. Don't tell your mother, or the people of the village until I have returned to my home, or they may try to spoil the happiness of my new life."

For several days Ngosa stayed in the village, helping her sister with her daily tasks until one day the mother asked the child how she was able to do her work so quickly by herself. "My big sister helps me, though I can't see her," the child replied, and she told her mother of Ngosa's invisible visit.

The mother had grown sadder and sadder because she had thrown her elder daughter out into the storm, and she called out loudly, "Daughter! Forgive me for driving you from your home. Come back, wherever you are, to those who love you." At her words the magic spell was broken, and Ngosa stood in front of her mother, able to be seen by all her family, though her father was too lazy even to look.

Her mother wept for joy as she took Ngosa back into the family. For many days the python waited patiently for his wife's return and, as the days passed, his loneliness increased. Finally he could bear it no longer and he left his water-home to find her.

As he slithered up the village pathway, the villagers fled away in panic. He reached the mother's hut and there he found his beloved wife. "Ah, my loved one," he whispered to her, "come back to me. My river-home is crying out for you." Then, turning to the mother he said, "Woman, you threw your daughter out of your home. You cannot take her away from me now, for I love her. She is my wife." Wiping the tears from his eyes, the snake husband sang,

> *"Day and night I am crying*
> *For my very own wife;*
> *The softest of beauties,*
> *The wife of my life.*
>
> *Storm rains come and help me,*
> *As you helped me before –*
> *Sweep down to the river,*
> *With the wife I adore."*

There were tears in Ngosa's eyes, too, as she realised how much the python loved her. She pleaded with her mother to let her return to her husband's underwater home. But the woman could not bring herself to part with Ngosa, so she drove the great snake away and shut the door. "I will send him presents," she said to herself, "and he will soon forget the child." Ngosa's father, needless to say, was too lazy to notice what was happening. So that night the woman filled a dish with delicious food and carried it down to the river where she placed it near the bank of the big, silent pool.

The python refused to be comforted, and throughout the night the breeze blew sorrowful cries up to the woman's hut. "I want my wife," he pleaded, "for she is the light of my eyes," and he left the food untouched.

"I will give him an even larger gift," said the mother, as she drove the few precious cattle that they owned down to the river and into the big, silent pool. But all through that night again came the same sad cry, blown to the mother's ears: "I want my wife, for she is the light of my eyes." And before morning broke, the big snake slithered into the hut where the family slept and, opening his enormous jaws, swallowed Ngosa once more.

Unharmed, as before, the python returned her to his underwater home. Never again was she seen by human eyes. To this day Ngosa lives in happiness with her loving python husband and his scaly subjects, beneath the silent ripples of the softly flowing river.

Narrator: N. O. Chilenge

THE ROOSTER AND THE SWIFT

MALAWI

The rooster Tambala, and his friend Nazeze the swift, thoroughly enjoyed light-hearted jokes and fun. Theirs was a happy friendship until their fun led to boasting, and their boasting turned to rivalry – each trying to make out that he was smarter than the other.

"Listen, my friend," said Tambala to Nazeze, after a long argument, "it takes a really good brain to present a successful trick, and my brain is easily better than yours."

"I will not agree to that!" argued the swift hotly. "You're just boasting! Let us have a competition and see which of us has the greater cunning. We'll invite everyone to a party, and our guests can act as judges to settle our argument once and for all."

The rooster agreed readily. So, for the next few days, each practised the trick that pleased him most. On the day of the party birds and animals from far and near gathered at the swift's house, looking forward to the entertainment, while judges were appointed to decide the winner. The swift was the first to show his skill. He had already told his wife to put a large pot of water upon the fire, and to have the water boiling. When the pot was bubbling merrily, Nazeze turned to his guests.

"Listen, everybody," he said. "This trick needs brains as well as speed. My friend Tambala here," and he pointed to the rooster, "says that he is cleverer than I. When he has done his trick, you must judge. I will now jump into this boiling water, and will come out quite unharmed. Watch!"

Without another word the swift disappeared into the dense cloud of steam that was rising from the furiously boiling water. As you know, the swift is called a "swift" because of the speed of his flight. So as he flew in circles under cover of the steam, his tremendous speed tricked them all, and no one saw him until, after about a minute or so, he flew out of the steam wet, but none the worse.

"There!" he said, turning to the rooster, "can you do that?"

"Of course I can – easily!" replied Tambala boastfully. "I can stay in the water twice as long as that!" and, strutting up to the pot he plunged head-first into the boiling water.

During the first minute that passed there was dead silence, and the excited circle of guests waited expectantly for Tambala to come out of the steam as the swift had done. But when he had failed to appear after double that time, they anxiously damped down the fire to find, when the steam had died down, a very dead rooster lying at the bottom of the big pot.

So you see, my friends, never boast that you can do a thing, unless you are quite sure that you can!

Narrator: Brighton Kumalo

THE PUNISHMENT
OF THE
FAITHLESS ONE

MATABELE

Although most bird-lovers know that the Trumpeter Hornbills of southern Africa make their nests in hollow tree trunks, it is not everyone who knows that, once the hen has laid her eggs, her husband seals the entrance with clay. He leaves only a small slit open through which he can pass food. So she is imprisoned inside the tree trunk until the young birds are old enough to be fed from outside. Then he breaks open the hole so that she can help him feed the fledglings.

If you ask the people of Matabeleland, they will tell you that the Hornbill cannot be blamed, for his wife richly deserves her imprisonment. It all started like this they say – in the days of long, long ago. The Hornbill and his wife used to build their nest in the treetops; they used twigs, well sewn together with hair from the tails of zebra and wildebeests. Inside, the nest was plastered with clay, and was lined with the softest thistledown.

They were a happy pair. Three fine eggs lay in their snug little home. Proudly the Hornbill sought the tastiest fruits in the forest, so that his dear wife need never leave the nest and the precious eggs. To find her favourite fruits, her devoted husband searched farther and farther away, which meant that the time he was away grew longer and longer.

Each day the dutiful wife turned the eggs beneath her, gently caressing their smooth white surface with her great beak. She had no thoughts beyond the joy of that first moment when her young ones would break from the shells that held them. But there was a wicked tempter abroad in the forest, in the form of a handsome bachelor who called softly to her from the treetops, trying to tempt her away from the eggs. At first she did not listen to this stranger but, as her husband was away for so long, she started to think wistfully of the days when she used to enjoy happy flights over green forests.

As soon as he saw her longing, the tempter increased his persuasion for her to join him on his joy flights. "One little flutter will not harm my precious eggs!" she thought. "Just one short flight with such a handsome companion! I will be back long before my husband returns."

What followed is not difficult to imagine. Every day, while the Hornbill husband searched the forest for dainties for his wife, she was flitting over the countryside with the gay-feathered bachelor. Day by day their pleasure-flights grew longer. One day the Hornbill found a big marula tree full of fruit nearby, that had escaped the notice of his sharp eyes in the past. Therefore, he was home much sooner than usual, his crop swollen with the delicacies that he had found for his beloved wife.

To his dismay he found their nest empty, and the three precious eggs barely warm. "What can have happened?" he wondered. "Has some dreadful monster carried off my dear wife?" Surely he would have heard her cries!

At least he could try to save the babies, he decided, by keeping them warm with his own body, and he settled down clumsily. He had been sitting on the eggs for only a few minutes when he heard laughter and merrymaking. "That is a voice I know," he said to himself. Then, into sight flew his wife and the handsome male Hornbill. The husband flew upon this intruder with rage, and there is still talk among the birds of the fierce battle that followed. The wicked tempter was put to flight as he deserved and driven far away, while the faithless wife returned in disgrace to her nest. But she had been away too long this time, and there was no warmth nor life in the eggs.

Carefully the guilty wife hid the truth from the Hornbill as, week after week, she sat upon the lifeless eggs. When, eventually, no chickens hatched her husband guessed the dreadful truth. He chased his guilty wife from the nest and one by one he flung the eggs to the ground, then he set about destroying their lovely treetop home completely. Next he looked for a tree trunk with a conveniently large hole in it, and inside this he made his wife lay her next clutch of eggs.

When the last egg had been laid, he cemented his faithless wife securely into the tree trunk allowing only a small slit to remain open. And that, so they say, is why to this very day, the Trumpeter Hornbill imprisons his wife in her nest, only breaking away the plaster when his fledglings are ready to leave the nest.

THE FOUNDING OF A TRIBE

A TRUE STORY FROM THE AREA WHERE GRAHAMSTOWN NOW STANDS

In the days of long ago, when witchcraft and sudden death were all too common, the great chief Tshiwo ruled over a vast stretch of land and a large number of people.

But all was not well in that land, for Tshiwo's witch-doctors held even greater power than he, and they kept him in a constant state of fear by telling him, from time to time, that he was being bewitched by one of his subjects.

The chosen victim would always be one who possessed a fine herd of cows – or something else which one of the witch-doctors wanted. "The bones were thrown" each time, and the witch-doctors would point to the man they had chosen and declare that he was the one who planned against his chief.

The punishment was always the same – death, after which all the victim's wives and cattle were seized. In this way the witch-doctors grew rich, for they were given a good share of the man's possessions. As their wealth increased, their greed grew greater, and they were always on the look-out for a rich innocent man to kill.

As you can see, it was the witch-doctors rather than the chief Tshiwo who held the greater power, and this caused great fear among the chief's honest subjects.

The name of the executioner whose duty it was to carry out these death sentences was Kwane. He was a just and kindly man. True, he too, made a profit from the killings, and his herd increased with every man he clubbed to death. But each cow that joined his flock in payment for the killings, brought deeper sorrow to his heart. He came to hate each journey to "The Place of Death".

As time wore on, he loathed his job more and more. His kindly heart told him that it was wicked to take the lives of those he knew had done no wrong.

The killing ground was far from the Royal Kraal. It was a wild and lonely rugged kloof, that was feared by all as a place of death and sorrow. No one ever went that way.

One day the witch-doctors "smelled out" a young and particularly handsome man and said he was guilty of trying to bewitch his chief. One of the witch-doctors probably wanted his lovely wife, or maybe his herd of fat cattle – so he, too, was sentenced to death and sent to the killing ground with Kwane.

The man was full of the joy of living; he did not want to die. All along the path to "The Place of Death" he begged Kwane to spare his life. Kwane knew this would be a dangerous thing to do, for if it ever became known that he had disobeyed his ruler, he too, would die. His own flocks and wives would be handed to the human vultures who were tricking his chief.

However, Kwane could not bear the thought of killing this strong and innocent man, so he tried to make a plan. "If I leave you alive," he asked, "where will you live? As you know, I risk my life if you are ever found."

"Yes, I know the risk you run," replied the young man, "but life is good: I do not want to die. I will give you my solemn word that I will stay here and never leave this place of death. No one will ever know that you showed me mercy."

So Kwane spared the young man's life, and he built himself a hut in that wild and lonely kloof. He lived by the skill of his hands on creatures that he snared, wild fruits and berries, and roots of many kinds.

From that day onwards, Kwane never killed another living soul. Each man, as he was sentenced to death by Tshiwo, was taken to "The Place of Death" and there Kwane released him and made him give the same promise of silence.

As time went on, Kwane smuggled grain to plant in the growing settlement, so that before long they had created small gardens, and lived their lives there in peace.

Eventually their numbers increased to over a hundred strong and healthy men – for the greedy witch-doctors were declaring more and more innocent men to be guilty. However, in spite of all their pretended skill, these wicked men could not prevent disaster from overtaking Tshiwo, and one day fighting broke out against a neighbouring tribe.

The battle was a bitter one, and Tshiwo's men were badly beaten: not many escaped with their lives. It was then that Kwane came forward and offered to help his chief.

"What can you, one man alone, do to help me?" asked the dejected chief. "I can bring you a hundred strong men," the old man replied.

"Bring them," ordered Tshiwo. "If they are fresh and willing, we might still save the day, for our enemies have not yet recovered from the fight."

Kwane went to the lonely kloof, and brought back with him all the men whom he had spared. Tshiwo was astonished to see so many of the men who were supposed to be dead, but gladly accepted their service. Without giving his enemies a chance to reorganise, he went into battle once more. This time, thanks to Kwane and his men, Tshiwo gained a great victory.

When the fight was over, the old chief called Kwane to him and willingly forgave him for his years of disobedience. What is more, he made him chief over the men he had saved, declaring that they had been more useful to him than all his wicked witch-doctors.

Throughout Kwane's lifetime, this new tribe called itself "The Children of Kwane", but when, sometime after his death, his grandson Cungwa became chief, they took the name of "The Children of Cungwa".

The tribe fought many fierce battles against the British before they put down their arms to become the civilized and peaceful people they are today.

Narrator: Blasins Kattlana, a direct descendant of Kwane

THE GUARDIANS
OF THE DEW POND

LESOTHO

A serious drought was troubling the land where the elephant ruled as king. The rivers and the waterholes were dry, and all the animals were suffering. King Elephant therefore called his subjects to a meeting. "We must build a dam," he told them, "to catch the dew at night. Then, at midday, everyone who has helped will be allowed to drink his share."

All through the day they dug, scraped, stamped and smoothed, until by night time, they had made a strong and gently sloping bowl to catch the dew.

Now one animal, the lazy, trouble-making hare, refused to lend a hand. He just sat on a big rock and laughed as the others sweated and toiled in the heat of the summer sun. That made the angry creatures promise that they would not allow him to drink one drop of water. They would take it in turns to guard the pond.

On the first day it was the owl's turn to see that the hare did not drink the water. But as you know, an owl's eyes are made to see by night, and in the sunlight he can't see so well at all. Therefore, when the cunning hare crept stealthily along, disguised by some dry grass on his back, the owl did not see him. He drank all the water in the pond, leaving the thirsty animals only mud to suck. That put the owl in great disgrace.

On the following day it was the dassie's turn to guard the pond. He took up his position on a little ant-heap nearby and, full of enthusiasm, he began to watch. Presently the hare arrived and without a word began to dig a hole with a little tunnel leading from it. Inside this he built a fire. The dassie was intrigued and said, "Tell me, friend, why are you doing that?"

"I am making a fire so that you and I can play the 'cooking game' ", replied the hare. "First you must cook me, and then I will cook you." And he made off towards the forest. There he found a pod from a creeper which made a loud popping noise when he squeezed it.

"Now," he said when he came back, "I will go inside the hole. When you hear me 'pop' you will know that I am cooked, and you must come and take me out. Then I will cook you. This game is great fun!" and he skipped into the hole.

After a short while there was a loud "pop" and the hare called, "I am cooked! Come and take me out!"

The dassie did as he had been told, and they both sat on the edge of the hole and laughed. Then the dassie, who agreed that it was a splendid game, jumped into the hole for his turn to be cooked.

But the hare had stoked up the fire in the tunnel before he left it, and very soon the dassie found it uncomfortably hot. He called out, "I am cooked now! Come and take me out!"

But the hare said, "Oh no! you have not popped yet. How can you be cooked?" Then he blocked up the hole with earth and stamped on it, until the poor dassie was suffocated. Once again, the hare drank all the water, and even cut off one of the dassie's ears to make a whistle for himself. When the animals came for their drink at midday, they again found nothing but mud in their dew pond.

Next morning it was the turn of the tiny buck, the "dik-dik", to guard the pond, and he took up his position near the water. Soon the hare came running out of the forest blowing on the whistle he had made, and dancing as he ran. He went up to the dik-dik, who was delighted by the noise, and said, "Let's have a game. I'll play on my whistle while you dance, and then you can play on it while I dance." He played such a catchy tune that before long they were both dancing, and thoroughly enjoying themselves.

Then the hare handed the whistle to the little buck and said, "Your turn now. I will dance by myself."

The dik-dik was so pleased with his new toy, and played it with such joy that he did not notice the hare dancing nearer and nearer to the pond. Finally he reached it, and quickly drank up all the water. The animals were angrier than ever when once more they had to go without their midday drink.

It was then that the tortoise asked if he could be left on guard the following day. All the animals readily agreed, for he was known to be an honest fellow, and was admired for his wisdom and his cunning.

He went very stealthily to the forest before it was light next morning, and smeared a strong layer of sticky sap from one of the forest trees, on his back. Then, making himself look as much like a stone as possible, he waited in the middle of the path at the water's edge.

Presently the hare came tripping along the path singing to himself, looking around to see if there was anyone on guard, and wondering how he should trick him this time? There seemed to be no one on guard, and nothing but some stones in the pathway, so he hopped from stone to stone until he was standing on the tortoise himself. There he bent down to drink.

"Got you at last!" cried the tortoise, as the hare's lips touched the water.

The hare stood up and tried to turn round to see who had spoken, but he could not lift his feet from where he was standing!

They were firmly stuck to the tortoise's back, and how the tortoise laughed at his struggles!

The glue held fast, and the more he struggled, the more frantic the hare became. Anyway, that was where the animals found him when they came for their midday drink.

They beat the wicked hare and then strung him up by his arms to a high tree, promising to kill him the next morning.

Now, the jackal who had been away working in his tobacco fields for a week or so, knew nothing of the hare's tricks, and shortly after sun-up on the following morning he happened to pass the tree where the hare hung by his paws. "Hullo!" exclaimed the jackal in surprise, "whatever are you doing up there?"

"I'm playing a wonderful game," replied the hare. "Come and play with me. It's much more fun with two."

"All right," answered the jackal, who was always ready for a bit of fun. "What shall I do?" "First undo this rope, and I will pull you up beside me," answered the hare. The jackal did so, and in no time the hare had hauled him up and tied him by the paws in his place. "Bye!" called the hare, with a rude laugh, and left him. And when the animals arrived later in the morning to punish the wicked hare, all they found was one sore jackal instead.

THE MISCHIEF MAKER

KIKUYU

For many years a lion and a jackal had been devoted friends. Each had his own private hunting ground in the forest, and when he had made a kill, he would call loudly for the other to join him. They would then eat and chat happily together and discuss the news of the forest.

But Sunguru the hare was highly jealous of this friendship, because they hadn't invited him to join them. So he planned to make mischief between them. "I'll put one against the other," he decided, and it was not long before he thought out a plan.

The next time that he saw the two friends set out for their hunting-grounds, Sunguru hid between the two areas and waited. Before long he heard the lion call, "Friend, friend, come quickly! I have found some honey."

Imitating the jackal's voice as well as he could, the hare called back, "Eat by yourself. I'm tired of being friends with you!"

The lion was most upset when he heard what he thought was his friend. He did not understand why the jackal should be so rude. However, he went sadly on his way and said nothing. So all that day and for several days after, the jackal listened in vain for his old friend's voice.

Sunguru stayed in hiding between the two hunting-grounds, and eventually the jackal made a good kill after which he called loudly to his friend, "Lion, lion, come quickly and eat with me! I have killed a bush pig."

"Then eat it alone! I don't want to be friends with you," the hare called back in a voice as much like the growl of a lion as his small throat could manage. The jackal could hardly believe his ears. "How can an old companion treat me like that?" he muttered sorrowfully to himself. "One day I'll get my own back."

Life was now very lonely for the two animals. Each one wandered about on his own until one day the lion could bear it no longer. "There must have been a mistake!" he said to himself. "I'm going to call my friend over the next time I have something to share." So the very next time he found some food, he swallowed his pride and called out, "Friend jackal, come and share!"

However, Sunguru was still stirring up trouble, so he replied loudly in the jackal's voice, "Eat alone, I tell you! I don't need your friendship!"

This time the lion was very angry. "Wait until I meet that jackal!" he snarled. "I will kill him for treating me like that."

The jackal was equally annoyed when he too found his attempt to heal the friendship was answered with another insult. The two friends drifted farther and farther apart, each furious with the other – until they met accidentally one day in another part of the forest.

The lion bared his fangs and prepared to attack the jackal who promptly backed down an ant-bear hole. From there, he decided he could safely tell the lion what he thought of his rude behaviour.

As they listened to each other's story, it wasn't long before they realised that someone had planned to make mischief between them. "We must find out who it is," said the lion. So they decided to go to their own hunting-grounds, where the lion would once more call the jackal to his kill. The jackal would be waiting to catch whoever answered.

It did not take long before they heard the hare answering rudely as before, but the hare found himself caught as the jackal crept up quietly behind him. The lion joined the jackal, and they told Sunguru angrily that they were going to kill him then and there for his treachery (which they did). After that they made a vow to hunt his children and his children's children for evermore. And that explains why the jackal hunts the hare to this very day, and the lion continues to call the jackal to his kill.

Narrator: Gwida Mariko

THE HARE AND THE REEDBUCK

ZAMBIA

Good looking wives were scarce where the hare and the reedbuck lived. One day the two animals decided to make a journey together and search for the right type of wife.

As you may (or may not) know, it is the plump and well-rounded wife who fetches the greater marriage price and, as they walked along, the reedbuck boasted that he would naturally be looked upon as the wealthier of the two, and would therefore have the better choice.

"Nephew," he said, "I'm looking for a nice fat girl; one with big buttocks and strength in her arms. But who will ever marry you? No sensible girl would ever marry such a skinny creature. All you'll get will be an equally skinny wife who will only have the strength to scratch the earth to sow your crops. Oh, ho, ho!" and he laughed most unpleasantly at the hare.

However, the hare assured the reedbuck that he would go on searching until he did find a fat bride. So, after three days, they arrived at a village where there were many beautiful girls, and there they decided to stop, for the choice of brides was magnificent.

The girls were full of grace and beauty, their huts were clean and tidy, and the ripening grain from their fields was bursting with plenty. The hare and the reedbuck rested, and looked around.

Before long, the reedbuck called an old man and, giving him a love token, begged him to approach the parents of one of the maidens and make an offer of marriage, as was the custom.

Because some little time had passed and the old man had still not returned, the hare laughed at the reedbuck. "No wonder she doesn't want you: you eat only green beans from their gardens!" And he laughed loudly.

The reedbuck was annoyed. "Be quiet, will you?" he said. "Have you no respect for your uncle?" But just then the old man returned, with the news that the parents had accepted the reedbuck's request for their daughter's hand.

"Ah!" smirked the reedbuck to the hare. "Your tongue ran ahead of you! You spoke too soon of the way the wind would blow, we'll see what happens when your turn comes. My wife is strong and plump."

"Yes," agreed the hare, "you are indeed fortunate. With such a wife, people will bow down before you when you take her back to our village."

Before long the wedding preparations began, and a cow was killed to provide meat for the marriage feast.

"I too am going to find a wife!" said the hare.

So he went to the same old man, and asked him to go to the parents of a particularly plump girl whom he had been watching, and tell them that he had spoken to their daughter, that she was in love with him, and wanted to marry him. (This, of course, was a lie!)

"What!" gasped the girl, when her parents asked her. "Marry that skinny little runt? Why, I have never even spoken to him!" The same thing happened each time the hare tried to find a bride. The girls laughed at him and turned him down, because he was so small and skinny, and his envy of the reedbuck's good fortune grew and grew.

As the time for the reedbuck's marriage drew near, the hare began to think out plans for his uncle's downfall until he finally hit upon what he thought was a splendid idea. Late one night, a couple of days before the wedding, he crept stealthily into the goat pen belonging to the father of the reedbuck's future bride, and killed several of his goats. He drained the blood from one of these into a gourd and removed its skin. Then he went quietly to the reedbuck's hut, where he found uncle reedbuck in a very deep sleep. With great care he smeared him well with goat blood, and covered him with the skin.

By this time the remaining goats, smelling the blood of their companions, began to bleat, so the villagers came out of their huts to see what had happened. Everyone, that is, except the reedbuck, who was such a heavy sleeper that no amount of noise ever woke him.

The hare quickly mixed with the crowd, and when the dead goats were discovered, he exclaimed, "Oh, this is dreadful. I must tell my uncle reedbuck what has happened. He may be able to catch the culprit." He asked the father of the reedbuck's bride to accompany him, as he said he was afraid to go alone.

By the light of blazing torches they went to the reedbuck's hut and, pushing the door aside, went in. There they saw him asleep in a pool of blood with the skin of a freshly killed goat covering him.

"Oh! this is even more dreadful," cried the hare, as an angry crowd gathered at the door and shouted for the reedbuck to be killed. Time and again the poor reedbuck protested that he was innocent, but the proof was there for all to see, and the blood and the skin seemed proof enough of his guilt.

He was beaten severely, and driven from the village in disgrace, while everyone praised the clever hare for finding the killer of the goats so quickly.

In fact, the bride's father was so grateful that he gave his plump daughter to the hare as a reward. And that was how the hare, with many chuckles at his own cunning, married the reedbuck's bride.

THE JACKAL
BUILDS A HUT

LESOTHO

One day the animals asked the jackal, who was well known for his skill as a builder, to build them a house where they could gather together and enjoy themselves. He was happy to do so and set to work with a will. He worked hard, and soon had the walls up and the roof timbers in place.

Then he gathered the grass, and had started to thatch it when the hare came sauntering past. "Hullo, old friend," said the hare, "isn't it difficult, doing all that thatching by yourself?"

"Very," answered the jackal, pushing a large thatching needle through the grass, and carefully sewing it on to the rafters.

"Surely two can do it better than one?" asked the hare. "Let me go inside and push the needle back to you. I am always happy to help a friend."

"Thank you," said the jackal gratefully, "that is good of you. It will be a great help." So the hare went inside the hut and climbed up to the roof, where he began to help the jackal to sew the thatch.

Now the hare was not really trying to be helpful; he had a very different idea in mind. Presently he saw a chance. With great care he pulled the jackal's tail through the thatch and firmly sewed it with the grass to the rafters.

Knowing that the jackal was now quite unable to jump down from the roof, the wicked hare went outside and took the pot of food that the jackal had left bubbling on the fire. He carried it to where the jackal could see him and began to eat it with much smacking of his lips. "Look at me eating!" he called up. "My! it tastes good. Aren't you coming to join me?"

The jackal had gone to a great deal of trouble to prepare that stew, and he didn't want to share it with anybody. So he shouted, "Leave my stew alone!" But he could not move from where he was: his tail was too securely sewn to the rafters. No amount of pulling would loosen it.

The hare then climbed onto the roof and killed the poor jackal, after which he carefully skinned him. Then, putting on the jackal's skin over his own, he sat down once more beside the pot of stew and continued his meal.

While he was enjoying his stolen feast, the jackal's brother came walking past and thought he recognised his own brother. So he called out, "Good morning brother! We haven't seen each other for a long time. May I join you at your meal?" He was carrying a bag over his shoulder, and he put this down on the ground beside him.

"What have you got in there?" asked the hare, pointing to the bag after they had been talking for a while.

"Dagga," whispered the jackal's brother. "There's a good price for such stuff. Don't breathe a word to anyone, but there is plenty more of it in my fields!" he added with a sly wink.

"Oh dear!" cried the hare, pretending to look up in alarm, and keeping the jackal's skin round him, "the house that I am building is falling on us. Come quickly, and help me to hold it up!"

Obligingly, the second jackal rushed to put his paws against the wall that he thought was collapsing, and pushed with all his strength.

"Whatever you do don't let go, or it will fall and kill you," advised the hare as he picked up the bag of dagga and slung it over his shoulder. Then off he went, well pleased with himself. Of course the dead jackal's brother was much too afraid of being crushed, to leave off holding up the wall.

Needless to say, the hare had every intention of making a good profit from his stolen bag of dagga so that's the last we shall see of him. And the dead jackal's brother may still be there, holding up the wall of the hut.

THE WICKED CANNIBAL

KWAZULU

While their father worked in a faraway country, little Ncinci and her brother Mvemve lived with their mother in the hills of KwaZulu.

Maluzwane was a good mother. Her hut was clean and neat; her little ones were plump, and glossy from the lion fat that was rubbed into their strong young bodies each week. Lion fat, of course, was scarce, but everyone knew that the fat of the "Great One of the Forest" was good medicine for strength and beauty. Maluzwane did everything she should for the little ones.

Clothes were the least of her worries. Ncinci wore a little beaded string skirt. Mvemve was even easier to clothe, for he wore nothing at all.

They played every day with their friends, modelling small clay oxen, bathing in the nearby river, trapping birds – in fact, all the games that small black children play.

One day the girls and the boys went off to play in different directions. Ncinci and the other girls decided on some river games and went to bathe. The boys took a bag of grain to use as bait, and went to trap birds in the nearby hills, to roast for their midday meal.

Soon there came shouts of fun and laughter from the river as the girls tumbled about in the water and ducked each other; while from the hills arose a long, thin spiral of smoke as the boys started a fire on which to roast the birds they caught.

While the fun was at its highest, little Ncinci's string skirt came undone, and the woven string and wooden beads went floating down the river, bobbing and swirling as the swiftly running water carried them away.

"Oh!" she cried, "my lovely new skirt!" She turned to the girl nearest to her and said, "Please help me to catch it, before it is lost."

But her little friend replied, "That's nothing to do with me."

Ncinci turned to one of the bigger girls and said, "Please help me to catch my skirt. Your legs are longer than mine."

However, the older ones wouldn't help her either, and the string skirt bobbed farther and farther away. Ncinci began to weep, and ran splashing through the shallow water after it. But it always escaped her.

Once her hand was on it, but a wicked swirl of water swept it away from her fingers.

"Oh no!" she cried, "the water is holding me back. My legs move faster on the land." She scrambled up the bank and ran across to a shallow ford she knew around the river bend, to wait for her skirt to come floating by.

By this time she was out of sight of her friends and too concerned about rescuing her pretty little skirt to notice a tall black man with a big bag slung over his shoulder walking down the riverbank.

"Why are you running so fast, my little one?" asked the stranger.

"Please help me get my skirt!" she begged, pointing to where it bobbed up and down as the current carried it on.

"That is easy," he replied, striding into the water. In a moment he had it in his hand, and little Ncinci danced with pleasure as he brought it to her.

But as she stretched up her hand to take it, the stranger caught her roughly and pushed her into his bag. Too terrified to scream, she realized that she had been captured by one of the dreaded cannibals who were always on the lookout for children who strayed alone.

"Please, please, let me out," she pleaded.

"Oh, no," he replied. "it is long since I found one as plump as you. At home there's a fire ready crackling for my evening meal." He slung her over his shoulder and left the river behind him as he climbed the hills.

But Ncinci was heavy and he was hungry, so when he saw a long thin spiral of smoke climbing to the skies, he thought he would go that way and maybe beg a bite of food.

Soon he reached a slanting rock where Mvemve and his friends were roasting the birds they had caught. Seeing there were only children there, he marched boldly up to them and said, "Good morning, little brothers. I have come from far away, and I haven't eaten for a long time. Let me share your food and I in return will make my magic bag sing."

Now, every black child loves magic of any kind, so the boys shared their meal with the tall stranger, and when they had eaten, asked for their reward.

He went up to the bag and prodded it with his finger saying, "Sing, bag, sing."

That made Ncinci call out, "I am Ncinci, I am Ncinci, and my brother is Mvemve, my brother is Mvemve."

"Yours is a wonderful magic," said Mvemve, cleverly hiding his surprise at hearing his sister's voice. "Magic like that is worth more than these few roast birds. If you will come with me to my mother's home, she will give you a juicy steak from the ox she killed yesterday. I will run ahead and ask her to have food ready for you." And he raced down the hillside to warn his mother about the cannibal. So, by the time the cannibal reached her hut, Maluzwane had made her plans. She greeted him with what seemed to be a warm welcome, suggested that he put his heavy bag in the shade of a nearby tree, and asked him to fetch some water in a can for her to cook his meal.

As soon as he left for the river, Maluzwane quickly opened the bag, took Ncinci out and hid her in the goat pen. She then ran to a swarm of bees that hung from a nearby tree, popped the bag over them, shook them carefully inside, and tied it up once more.

She quickly hung the bag from the rafters of her hut, and as soon as the smoke from the fire had made the bees stupid and drowsy, put it back under the tree.

Now when the cannibal dipped the can which Maluzwane had given him into the river, he found that the bottom was full of holes. It took him some time to find the clay, and one by one he plastered up the holes.

When at last he reached the cooking hut, all was ready for the feast, and having eaten his fill, he once more slung the bag over his shoulders and, bidding his hostess goodbye, continued on his way.

"Wife," he called out as he neared his home, "bring our largest cooking pot and plenty of firewood, while I prepare a feast. Come in and close the door," he continued as his wife and child followed him into the hut.

He put down the load at the entrance, and while he sharpened a wicked-looking knife, he told the child to carry the feast into the hut. But no sooner had the child touched the bag, then the bees stung him through the cloth, and with a cry of pain he dropped it, and refused to touch it again.

"Very well," said the cannibal, "I will feast alone. Get out, both of you!" and he chased both mother and child away. He locked the door and, with wicked, gloating eyes, he himself undid the string that fastened the bag.

The bees were now awake and very angry. They flew straight to his head, and there they settled, and there they stung him as he tried wildly to unfasten the door.

Eventually he got outside, and with screams of pain, raced off to a muddy pool. Into the sticky mud he plunged his burning head. And there he stuck, feet in the air. And there the mud choked and suffocated the wicked cannibal, while the mother and son laughed with glee!

Narrator: Manalimeni Mkhize

NABULELA

KWAZULU

Nabulela was a huge long-toothed monster who lived in a small lake not far from a village in KwaZulu. Everyone feared him, so to keep him in a good temper, the villagers used to make flat porridge cakes, and place them at the water's edge at sunset for the great beast to eat. As they did so, they sang,

"Nabulela, Nabulela, come out and eat me.
Mahlevana the chief has said,
'Come out and eat me.'"

And then they would run away because Nabulela's favourite food was human flesh, and no one wanted to be caught and eaten alive.

But their chief, Mahlevana, had no thoughts of monsters. He had something else on his mind. For many years he had longed for a daughter, but his wives had borne him only sons. So when his favourite wife at long last presented him with a laughing, black-eyed girl, he was overjoyed. There was dancing and feasting in the royal kraal for many days, and all the countryside rejoiced.

She was named Hlalose which means "little princess", and as she grew from a baby to a girl, Mahlevana gave her all that her heart could desire. He dressed her with the gayest beads and she became the prettiest girl in all the land.

As time passed, however, all Hlalose's playmates became very jealous of her. Their love turned to hatred as they watched all the gifts she was given, though they were careful to hide this from both Hlalose and their chief.

One day, when she was seven years old, the children from the royal kraal went to play at a nearby river, and, as they reached the river's edge, they saw a tiny paw waving feebly from the water.

Her little playmates laughed to see a paw foolishly waving in the air, but Hlalose waded quickly into the pool to investigate. There she found a tiny mongrel puppy with a stone tied round its neck, almost drowned. As fast as she could, she took it to the riverbank where she nursed it back to life. Then she carried it gently to her father's hut.

"What are you carrying, my child?" Mahlevana asked, as his daughter carefully laid the puppy down.

"One of your people wanted to drown this little creature," she answered, "but I saved it. Now its life is part of mine."

She called the puppy Mpempe, and as time passed they loved each other more and more. They were never apart, and Mahlevana knew that no harm would come to Hlalose with Mpempe close at hand.

The years passed, and Hlalose grew into a beautiful happy maiden and Mpempe into an old and feeble dog – too old to follow his beloved mistress daily to fetch the water from the spring. So she used to leave him tied to her father's hut.

It happened one day, that all the girls were sent with earthen pots on their heads to the clay pits, to fetch the red ochre to smear on their faces for the tribal dance. Mpempe wanted to follow, but the pits were far away, so Hlalose tied him as usual to the hut and, singing the Clay Pot Song, she joined the laughing throng. When they reached the clay pits, the girls gaily reached down and pulled up lumps of the red clay to fill their pots.

As Hlalose's beauty and good humour had grown through the years, so had the jealousy of the other girls. So, on this special day, they whispered among themselves, and made a plan.

As Hlalose bent down to pull up a last handful of clay from the bottom of the pit, they grabbed her roughly and pushed her in. Then they covered her up with the earth that lay around the pit, and left at once for home.

When they came in sight of the kraal, the dog jumped up to greet his beloved mistress. But when all the girls had gone by and he could give no bark of welcome, he began to whine instead. The darkness was falling so they all went in to eat their evening meal.

At first only the dog noticed that Hlalose was not there, but when the chief returned to his hut, he found the thong chewed through, and Mpempe gone.

This is strange," he said. "Where is my daughter and why has Mpempe gone?"

No one knew. "No, she did not go with us," lied the clay gatherers. "We heard her speaking of some man she wanted to meet at the waterhole," and they hurried away to bed.

Then, as the chief called men to light torches and begin a search, Mpempe staggered into sight.

His legs and head were plastered with clay, and in his mouth was a leather thong tied to a little wooden amulet that Hlalose always wore.

"Ah," said the chief, "the girls have lied to me. Carry the faithful Mpempe. He will show us where to look. See the clay on his body! To the clay pits! Hurry!" Off they went in haste, with blazing torches carried high.

As the clay pits came into sight, the dog started to whine, and then there was a shout of joy from a high tree. There sat Hlalose in its topmost branches.

The chief saw proof of what had happened – the hole in which Hlalose had been buried, with claw marks all around where Mpempe had dug his mistress out; and the smears and smudges all over her face where he had licked her back to life.

"Then we heard the lions roar," cried his daughter, and I climbed the tree." There, sure enough, were large marks of the big cats' paws as they had prowled around the tree.

"But when they saw the flames from the torches as you came, the lions ran away. I dropped the amulet as I climbed the tree. Mpempe seized it and ran to fetch you. Now he has saved my life."

Next morning, Mahlevana called the clay gatherers to him and said, "Those who give death, receive death, but because Mpempe gave Hlalose the chance to live, I will give each of you a chance to live. For a long time now it has been my wish to wear the snow-white skin of the great fierce water beast, Nabulela. Bring it to me, and I will spare your lives."

The girls looked at each other in dismay. They had been given a fearsome task. Which should they try to do? To take Nabulela alive, or kill him?

Their hearts sank at the thought. However, they made their plans, and they all set out that afternoon, with a big pot of the usual porridge cakes.

They took care, however, to leave the strong, circular cattle kraal open at each end, and they also left four of their number to guard the gates, two at either entrance. Then off the others went, to Nabulela's home.

As the lake came in sight they began their song,

> "Nabulela, Nabulela, come out and eat me.
> Mahlevana the chief has said,
> 'Come out and eat me.'"

Soon out of the water came an enormous mouth ready to receive the offering. But as the mouth opened wide, the girls saw two toothless jaws, and they knew that this was not the right creature. So they picked up their porridge cakes, and continued round the lake, still singing their song to call Nabulela to his feast. Many creatures appeared but not one of them was Nabulela.

At last, as darkness descended, there arose from the water a snow-white creature, and in his open mouth huge teeth gleamed. Yes, this was the beast they wanted.

The girls went on singing their song, and started gently drawing farther and farther from the water's edge, pulling the cakes with them while Nabulela followed.

When the fearsome beast was right out of the water, they dropped the cakes and ran for home, and Nabulela chased after them. They ran as fast as they could, but the great beast's legs were strong, and he ran faster. Slowly and surely he gained on them.

Just as they felt they could run no further, the village came in sight. They ran straight through the cattle kraal and as they passed through the farthest gate, their friends pushed in the heavy posts just ahead of Nabulela who was sniffing at their heels. He turned back to the gate where he had come in, but that had been closed behind him, and he found himself a captive in the big round kraal.

Then came the fathers of the girls with shields and gleaming spears to finish their daughters' work and save them from the chief's anger. They were too many for the great beast and at last Nabulela sank bleeding to the ground.

So it was that until his death Mahlevana wore Nabulela's snow-white skin as a cape across his shoulders, and the clay gatherers were forgiven.

And still today in the faraway villages in KwaZulu, the little ones ask for the song of Nabulela to soothe them to their slumber.

Struik Lifestyle
(an imprint of Random House Struik (Pty) Ltd)
Company Reg. No 1953/000441/07
The Estuaries, 4 Oxbow Crescent, Century Avenue, Century City 7441
PO Box 1144, Cape Town 8000, South Africa

www.penguinrandomhouse.co.za

First published by Struik Timmins (hardcover) in 1988
Second edition (softcover) published in 1991, Reprinted eight times
Third edition published by Struik Publishers in 2006, Reprinted in 2007.
Fourth edition published by Struik Lifestyle in 2014
Reprinted in 2017

ISBN 978-1-43230-342-6 (Print)
ISBN 978-1-43230-492-8 (PDF)
ISBN 978-1-43230-491-1 (ePub)

Fourth edition
Publisher: Linda de Villiers
Managing editor: Cecilia Barfield
Proofreader: Gill Gordon
Design manager: Beverley Dodd
Designer: Randall Watson
Illustrator: Gina Daniel

Reproduction by Hirt & Carter Cape (Pty) Ltd
Printing and binding by DJE Flexible Print Solutions, Cape Town